Black Fairy Tales

TERRY BERGER

Black Fairy Tales

drawings by David Omar White

Atheneum   1971   New York

This book was done especially
for the Black Children
who have never read
black fairy tales

COPYRIGHT © 1969 BY TERRY BERGER
THESE FAIRY TALES ARE ADAPTED FROM
Fairy Tales from South Africa BY E. J. BOURHILL
& J. B. DRAKE, MACMILLAN, LONDON 1908
ALL RIGHTS RESERVED
LIBRARY OF CONGRESS CATALOG CARD NUMBER 70-75517
MANUFACTURED IN THE UNITED STATES OF AMERICA
BY KINGSPORT PRESS, INC., KINGSPORT, TENNESSEE
DESIGNED BY JUDITH LERNER
FIRST PRINTING JULY 1969
SECOND PRINTING AUGUST 1970
THIRD PRINTING OCTOBER 1971

Contents

Black Fairy Tales

The
Moss-Green Princess
A SWAZI TALE

THERE WAS ONCE a little black Princess named Kitila, and she was both pretty and nice. Her father, a great chief, had been killed when she was but a babe, and now she and her mother lived with her uncle, who had become the new chief of the tribe. Unlike her father, who had been loved by all for his goodness, the new chief, his blood brother, was neither kindly nor popular.

Although he had made Kitila's mother one of his own Queens and Kitila, his Princess, he did not treat them as he should have. The tribe's love and continued loyalty to them made him fearful for his own position as King, and jealous of the two who were so popular.

The King had another wife besides Kitila's mother, and

that wife had given him a daughter whose name was Mapindane. It was this wife and her child that the King loved very much, and Kitila and her mother had only his deep and bitter hatred.

So strong was the King's dislike for Kitila and her mother that he did everything he could to show how much he despised them. He did not allow Kitila as much as one necklace of beads, and her little skin dress was always shabby and poor. His dislike for her was so great that he became enraged whenever she was admired.

And finally his hatred became so strong that he decided to cause her great shame. He decreed that Kitila must wear the skin of an ugly water beast, the Nya-Nya Bulembu. Long-toothed and sharp-clawed it was, and its skin was covered with bright green moss. By dressing her in the skin of this beast, the King felt sure that all of his people would fear her and no prince would ever come to love her.

To secure a Nya-Nya Bulembu skin, the King sent his bravest huntsmen out to search for the creature. This was no easy task because the animal was really a fairy beast with magic powers, and he made his home under the water. The King had instructed his men to fetch him an animal that was young, with regular teeth, long claws and a perfect skin, well covered with green moss. He also gave orders for plenty of green mealie bread to be made with which to entice the beast out of the water.

The party of selected hunters went out, and they followed the river until they came to a deep pool, where the water was quite black. Holding the green mealie bread with which to bait the beast, they stood in a circle and chanted the song of the Nya-Nya Bulembu:

"Nya-Nya Bulembu, Nya-Nya Bulembu,
Come out of the water and eat us!
The King has sent for the great Nya-Nya Bulembu!
Come and let us see you!
Laugh and show us your teeth!"

Out came a huge old monster, with only two or three teeth left, and no moss on his skin at all.

"No," said the huntsmen at once, "we don't want you."

They journeyed on again in a great storm of wind and rain. When it had passed away and the sun shone once more, they found themselves at a second big pool, which was as blue as the sky. Here they stopped and sang the song of the Bulembu once more. Out came a vicious-looking creature, with but little moss on his coat, and only one tooth three feet long.

"No, we don't want you either," said the huntsmen, and they traveled on again until they came to a third pool, which was bright green. Around it grew a most beautiful fringe of green moss, and the water itself was vivid green, like the grass in the spring.

Once more the huntsmen sang the magic song, and out came a nice green Bulembu, beautifully covered with moss, and showing all his long white teeth. The hunters placed big pieces of mealie bread for him, and as he came out to eat, they caught him alive. Then they traveled like the wind to the King's kraal. As they drew near home they sang:

"Have all your spears ready!
The Nya-Nya Bulembu is coming!"

All the men in the kraal seized their spears and hurried to the gate by which the Bulembu must enter. They stood in line in front of the entrance, and as the green monster rushed upon them, he fell on their spears and died. Then they took the body to the hut of the despised Queen and began to prepare the skin for use.

Cutting the body open, the men could hardly believe what they saw, for the most beautiful beadwork lay within the beast. There were necklaces and bracelets and little bags of every color and pattern. Never before had the villagers seen such beautiful work, and they took it out and brought it to the King. Then they removed the skin of the Bulembu very carefully, preserving the nails and all the teeth, and when the skin was quite complete they wrapped the little Princess Kitila in it.

The instant it touched her it fitted as if it were a part of her; indeed, she could not get it off again, for it was the skin of a fairy beast, as the King well knew. Kitila no longer looked like a little girl at all; instead she looked like a hideous green monster. She and her mother cried bitterly over this, but there was nothing to do about it. The King's order had to be obeyed.

Because the poor little Princess looked just like the

Bulembu himself, the people of the village feared her and stayed away from her, just as the King had hoped. Only the Princess Mapindane still played with Kitila, for both of these princesses had always been very fond of each other. They sat by themselves every day in the middle of the cattle kraal, the one in the green skin with long white teeth, the other in all the prettiest beads imaginable and a lovely little cloak of leopardskin, the finest the King could give her.

The years passed by, and the little girls grew into womanhood. Mapindane was now very lovely; she was a joy to behold as she sat in the sun, but poor Kitila was still clothed in her hideous green skin and looked as ugly as ever.

Now it happened one day that all of the villagers left the kraal in order to harvest their first fruits. Only Mapindane and Kitila were left behind, with one old Queen to watch over them. Suddenly a flock of birds appeared overhead. Swooping down, the birds seized the beautiful Princess and carried her away, but the green monster they left alone.

The old Queen looked up and shrieked, 'There goes the lovely Princess! There goes the King's favorite child!" She tried to call the villagers in from the fields, but the birds had risen so quickly into the air that before anyone came the birds were to be seen no more.

They flew and flew, far far to the North, carrying Mapindane to a faraway country. And there they dropped her in the kraal of a great King, not telling her what good fortune awaited her. For the King of that land fell in love with her and married her at once, and Mapindane had never been so happy.

The Princess could not send the good news to her father and mother, for no one in her new home had heard of her people, or even knew the way through the thick forests which lay between them. So her mother and father never knew of her good fortune, and they believed that the birds had eaten her.

Poor Kitila was worse off than ever, for the bereaved Queen was very jealous and angry; and as she was all-powerful, Kitila was no longer allowed to live as a Princess. She was forced to do all sorts of degrading work. At last the King said to her, "You are no good at all; you must go and scare the birds. You are so ugly that every bird that sees you will fly away at once." And he ordered that Kitila be sent at once to the fields to scare the hungry birds away from the crops, making her the village scarecrow.

From that day on the Princess was no longer called Kitila, but only Nya-Nya Bulembu. In her misery she often cried to her mother, "How hard my life is! Why was I born to such sorrow?" To this her mother always replied, "Do not despair; all will come out right." Her mother always reminded her that the Bulembu was a fairy beast and implored her to have faith in its magic powers.

One day on the way to the fields, Kitila met a very old man, whom she had never seen before. He came to her and handed her a stick saying, "When you get to the fields, just wave this stick and all the birds will fall dead at your feet without chasing them. When you go bathing, take the stick with you into the water; your own true body will reappear. Remember never to let go of the stick or the magic power will leave you."

Kitila took the stick from the old man, and everything happened just as he had told her. So she knew that he was truly a fairy in the shape of an old man. Now her job was easy. When she raised the stick in the fields, the birds fell to the ground and the crops were safer than they had ever been.

In the afternoons, when all the creatures were asleep, she went down to the river. As her foot touched the water, the green skin floated away, and hundreds of pretty fairies came to play with her. She stood in the water and sang:

> "Nya-Nya Bulembu, Nya-Nya Bulembu,
> Here I am!
> I was dressed like a monster,
> But I am like any girl.
> Now they feed me with the dogs."

Then she called for food, and instantly a fine feast appeared, and she and all of the Fairies ate and laughed together. But this happiness did not last long. For as soon as she came out of the river, her green skin reappeared, and once more she was Nya-Nya Bulembu.

One day some of the village children were playing on the hill and chanced to see the Nya-Nya Bulembu enter the water and immediately change into the beautiful Princess that she really was. They were so astonished that they ran back to the kraal to tell Kitila's mother what they had witnessed. She was delighted to hear their tale, but she begged them not to say a word about it to any of the others. And they did not.

Now it happened that some months later a great Prince came to visit the King. He was young and handsome, but he was noted above all for his wisdom and good judgement. His father had sent him in search of a bride. She was to be the most beautiful woman that he could find, and everyone waited anxiously to see what girl such a wise Prince would choose. The young man had traveled far and wide, but had found no maiden he could love. And, at last he had come to the kraal in which lived the Moss-Green Princess. He went directly to the King and asked him if he had any daughters.

"Yes," said the King, "but I have only one. I shall show her to you with pleasure."

"Yes, let the Prince see the monster," said Mapindane's mother, with a bitter laugh. So the Prince was taken to the fields where Kitila worked at scaring the birds. When he got there, he was astounded to find an ugly green monster walking through the fields with a stick upraised to frighten the birds away from the crops. He stood and watched the beast in horror, especially when he saw the birds fall dead. He was sure that some trick had been played upon him, but what he saw interested him too much to leave.

Suddenly the green beast started descending from the

10

fields, slowly moving toward the river. As the Prince watched, Nya-Nya Bulembu reached the pool and as she touched the water, the green skin fell away and there stood the loveliest maiden the Prince had ever beheld. At that instant he fell in love with her and solemnly vowed to make her his wife, no matter what spell she was under.

All that afternoon he stayed and watched her as she played with the Fairies in the cool green shadows. He longed to join them, but he did not dare. As he listened, he heard Kitila sing the story of her life, and then he understood everything.

At last he got up and returned to the kraal of the King. Here he shocked everyone by announcing, "I will marry your monster."

The King was surprised beyond belief, but he consented nevertheless. Preparations were made for the wedding, and a royal outfit was made for Nya-Nya Bulembu from the beautiful beadwork that had been found in the beast when it was captured. The Prince in the meantime returned to his father, who sent a gift of one hundred cows to the King, to show how much he esteemed the bride's hand. He also sent a fine head of cattle for her mother, as was the custom.

Then the Prince waited for the Moss-Green Princess to come to him, for in the land of the Kafirs, the marriage always takes place in the home of the bridegroom. His people waited too, in great expectation, for they were sure that their Prince had chosen the most beautiful maiden that could be found. It was with horror then that they beheld the strange green monster that arrived, with long white teeth and sharp claws, attended by four bridesmaids.

"What?" they asked. "Is this the peerless beauty chosen by our wise Prince? How can he marry such a monster?"

The poor Princess Kitila approached the hut of the Prince, trembling for fear she would not be admitted. She was sure that he would reconsider his offer of marriage and this time reject it as a bad bargain. To her delight, however, he kept his pledge despite her green skin and received her kindly. She was taken to a beautifully decorated hut, and early the next morning she was awakened to prepare for the wedding.

Now the Princess and her maids were instructed to go down to a deep pool in the nearby river to bathe. The sun had barely risen as they approached the water, and the air was fresh and cool. Nya-Nya Bulembu held the stick in her hand while she stepped into the pool. The minute she touched the water, as always before, the green skin fell away, but this time instead of floating on the water, it flew straight up into the sky. It was carried for many miles, until it came down right at the door of her mother's hut. Then the despised Queen knew that all was well, and that her daughter was happy at last.

When the Princess came out of the water, she was no longer Nya-Nya Bulembu, the moss-green beast. She was once again Kitila, a King's daughter, in her own true form. She returned to the kraal with her bridesmaids, all dressed in their wedding array, and there they were met by the women of the Prince's tribe. The horror these women had felt changed at once to joy and astonishment when they saw so lovely a Princess. Truly, they said, such beauty had never been seen among them before, and they praised the wisdom of their Prince, who had chosen such a magnificent bride.

The marriage ceremony took place with one of the happiest onlookers being Kitila's mother, whom the Prince had brought to his land as a surprise for his bride. And so the Princess Kitila lived among her husband's people in great happiness and honor. The story of her beauty became so famous that people came from many places just to look at her.

But the old King was well punished for his evil ways. For while he often heard of the happiness of Nya-Nya Bulembu, he never saw his favorite daughter again, and believed her dead.

The Serpent's Bride

A SHANGANI STORY

In the great wooded plains that lie between the mountains and the sea, there was once a most wonderful river. It was broad and deep, and its flow was outlined by great fig trees capped with white flowering thorns. You could always tell it from afar, in both summer and winter, for masses of evergreen foliage followed its many windings. The land through which it coursed was emerald green, and many herds of goats and sheep fed on the neighboring hills for the grass was sweet and good.

A powerful tribe had settled in this land, and on the side of a hill that sloped up from the riverbanks they had built a large city. There was plenty of wood and good water and all of the huts faced the morning sun. Because of this the mealie fields grew in abundance, extending as far down as the riverside.

The King of this tribe was the richest and most powerful man in the whole country, and his herds of cattle were a wonder to behold. Game was abundant, and the King who was a great hunter had decked his hut with many skins of lions and tigers.

Indeed, the King had only one trouble, but that was trouble enough. He and his people depended upon the river for their daily supply of water, and every now and again that water would suddenly cease to flow. The entire river would dry up, and this seemed to happen at any time of the year without warning. Sometimes the dryness would last for weeks, and the women would be forced to travel several hours in order to get fresh water from a distant stream. No one in the tribe could explain why this odd thing happened to the river, but nevertheless it continued to plague them.

Even stranger than the dry river, however, was the fact that there was one Princess among them who could always fill her calabash, no matter how dry the riverbed. She was the most beautiful of all the King's daughters; tall and graceful, with skin like flower petals and black eyes that danced like sun upon the water. Because she never went with her sisters to the river, no one knew where her water came from; everyone supposed that she had found some hidden pool that never quite dried up and that she did not wish to share this secret with them. Her name was Timba.

At the time of the story, the river had been flowing steadily for many months; the cornfields were in full ear, and the great tasseled mealies stood higher than a man's head. Every day all of the Princesses went down to the river to fetch water and to bathe in the great Red Pool. Only Timba went alone, but her sisters had long ceased to notice her love of solitude.

Then one day a strange thing happened. The morning was cool and fresh after a heavy thunderstorm and the tall grasses were drenched with raindrops. All of the maidens from the neighboring kraals came down to the river singing and laughing. There were tall, well-grown women and slender girls among them; and even little maids of five or six, each with a calabash on her head. They walked in single file, for the paths were narrow, and they shouted gaily to one another across the mealiefields. Only Timba remained silent as she walked behind her sisters; the last of the group.

At the riverside the women stopped abruptly, cries of dismay breaking from every mouth. For the bed of the stream was all but empty, and rocks that could not usually be seen, now stood high and dry. In a few hours the little water that still remained would disappear in the heat of the summer sun. With heavy hearts the girls followed the course of the stream to learn if any clear water could still be had. But none was to be found.

When they returned home, their calabashes were only half full of water, and that was muddy. Only the Princess Timba's water was as clear as crystal, and her jar was so full that she had placed branches of the white-flowering thorn around its brim to prevent it from spilling over as she walked.

The King was disturbed to learn that the river had failed once again. He put all his greatest magicians to work, promising unheard of rewards to anyone who could bring water back to the riverbed. Wisemen and rain doctors, from near and far, cast their magic spells; but though great storms arose and passed over the land, the riverbed remained empty, and even the deepest water holes dried

up. Only Timba continued to reap water from the river; and as often as she went down, so often would she return with a brimming calabash crowned with green leaves and her eyes bright and full of mysterious joy.

Finally her sisters could allow her to entertain her secret no longer. "Where do you get your water?" they queried.

And Timba answered, "I get it from the great King of the Waters, who rules the river and all of the streams that run into it, yes, even the tiniest creeks. He is angry now, and that is why the river is empty."

Her sisters were more puzzled than before. None of them had ever heard of such a King.

In the meantime the winter was approaching. Nights were growing colder, and the crops had to be gathered in. No rain would be falling now for many months, and the King and all his wise men knew that the riverbed would remain empty until spring. The tribe was in great trouble, for they and their cattle would surely die of thirst during the long dry season. Imagine their amazement then when one morning they found the river filled to overflowing, as if it were the season of summer floods. And yet, no rain had fallen in the entire country. The people did not understand, they could only rejoice in their wonderment. On that same day the beautiful Princess came running up from the river, laughing and singing as she called her sisters together.

"What is it? Tell us your news," they begged, for they saw that something exciting had happened.

"My dear sisters, I am going to be married!" said Timba joyfully.

"But to whom?" they asked. "No suitor has been here for months."

"To the great King of the Waters," she answered with pride.

"Who is he?" cried her sisters, "and where does he live? It must be very distant from here, for no one else has ever spoken of him."

Yet now Timba ceased to speak. To all other questions she only nodded her head mysteriously and muttered,

"Only I can know."

That same evening as the sun was setting, she slipped out of the kraal and started toward the riverbank. The little path was beaten down as hard and firm as the floor of a hut, for the mealies had long been gathered and no rain had fallen for a good long time. She passed the Red Pool, which was now full of water from one end to the other, and following the course of the river for half an hour or more, came at last to a great white thorn tree surrounded by a tangle of creepers and flowering shrubs. There she rested for a moment and then forced her way through the overhanging branches until she reached the water's edge. Standing there knee-deep among green lily pads, she looked out on a wide expanse of water. It was still and dark and very deep, and the current was barely visible on its smooth surface. A tiny crescent moon was hanging in the West, and its reflection quivered silver into the stream.

As Timba watched and waited, a sudden ripple broke toward the bank, spewing forth the head of a great serpent. All that could be seen was a deep, soft black, except for two red circles round his glittering eyes. He swam straight to the Princess, and she moved forward quickly and greeted him eagerly. Reaching the bank at last, he coiled himself beside her and his eyes shone with joy.

"Let us not wait any longer," he begged her. "Start making the preparations for our marriage. As midwinter approaches I will cause the river to rise twice in full flood, and then you will know that I am waiting for you."

And so until the little moon sank down and all the stars came out, they continued to sit and talk. Only then did the serpent rise up and swim down the stream, his head held high and his huge length extending far behind it.

This, then, was the King of the Waters who ruled the whole length of the great river. It was he who had courted the Princess both evenings and mornings as she came to fetch water. Now Timba stood watching him until he was out of sight, and then she returned to her home.

On the very next day Timba and all of her companions began to get ready for the wedding. Some of them wove mats out of golden-colored grasses: mats for sitting on and mats for grinding corn on, lest some of the meal fall on the ground and be wasted. Then there were the long mats made of bulrushes for sleeping on, which were only brought out at night. Other girls took lengths of thin cloth, bought from distant traders along the coast in exchange for ivory and horn, and these they fringed with strings of many colored beads. They were the cloaks for the bride, and as graceful and pretty as any dresses you could wish to see. Finally there were girdles to be made of colored beads, and many necklaces and dainty ornaments fashioned with twisted wire. After all Timba was a Princess and she was going to marry a King!

All these preparations took much time, and because it was winter, the days for working were short. For several weeks Timba had not had time to see her lover or even to go down to the river for that matter. But one morning, when the days were at their shortest, a young man came running in from hunting rabbits, shouting that the river was in full flood. Timba's heart pounded in her chest, for this was the first of the promised signs. She worked still harder now, and she hurried her maidens along, for she knew that only a few days remained before the second sign would appear.

At last all was ready, and the Princess started down to the river. The first flood had passed, and she walked slowly, searching the river to see if there were any signs of the second. Suddenly she heard a whistling call.

"Ping! Ping! Ping!"

She recognized the call of her bridegroom, but he was nowhere to be seen. She looked up the river once more, and this time she noticed that the stream was widening. Every moment it became fuller; great boulders that had been high and dry only a minute before were already half covered, and a dull roar could be heard from the distance. Now Timba knew for sure that the King of the Waters awaited his bride. Running home she sought out her bridesmaids.

"Come quickly," she begged them, "and bring along everything that we have made, but do not let anyone see us. The great King of the Waters is waiting for me at the river."

The bridesmaids ran hither and thither collecting all the pretty things that they had made, while the bride arranged herself for the marriage. In the Shangani country a bride wears a skirt of cotton cloth. Timba's wedding skirt was striped in red and blue. It reached to her knees, and above it she added a beautiful girdle of beads. Reaching for a cloak of dark blue cloth that was heavily fringed in red and white, she knotted it upon her left shoulder. This cloth was very thin and it hung in folds, revealing her graceful form. Last of all she placed beautiful beaded necklaces around her neck, and then covered her arms with bracelets, cunningly woven of shining brass and copper wires. When she was all finished dressing, it would have been difficult, if not impossible, to find a more lovely sight.

Carrying all of their handiwork, the maidens gathered together to start down hidden paths to the river. Not a word did they speak to anyone. When they reached the water, they stopped and called to one another in astonishment, for the river was in full flood, over half a mile wide. Great trunks of trees swept past in wild disorder, their branches tossing on the yellow waters. Now and then a dead buck floated by, and always huge boulders swept past amid a deafening roar. The girls hurried on to the Black Pool, where the water had already reached the lower branches of the great thorn tree. There they found that the sky overhead was surprisingly clear and cloudless.

"Never have I seen such a flood," said one. "Surely the river must be bewitched."

"There has been no rain for three months," cried another; "where can the waters have come from?"

They all turned to Timba for an answer, but she offered

them none. Instead she commanded them, "Leave everything here and return to your homes, but tell them nothing about this at the kraal!"

No sooner were the bridesmaids out of sight, than the serpent King lifted his great flat head from the water. As the Princess watched him, he grew taller and taller, until at last he stood upon his tail, towering above her. His head reached the top of the tallest tree, and his body stood straight like a shining black pillar. Fixing his bright eyes upon her, he said, "You must never be afraid of me, no matter what I do."

"I promise never to be frightened of you," she replied.

"Are you quite sure of that?" he asked her again.

"Quite sure," she answered firmly.

Satisfied, the serpent descended again and coiled himself beside her.

"And now," he said, "what of the lobola? I must send that to your father or the marriage will not be complete."

"Send the gift to the great cattle kraal," offered Timba. "When they see the oxen, they will understand that my marriage gift has come."

"Wait here," said the serpent; "I will return as the moon rises."

That very night he sent the cattle, and at daybreak it caused a great commotion in the city. The Princess had disappeared, and the air was full of strange bellowings, which came from the cattle kraal in the center of town. One hundred splendid oxen were discovered there; finer than anyone had ever seen. But strangely enough, not one person had seen the cattle arriving, and there was no trace of a herdsman. For many a long day, everyone talked about these mysterious doings.

In the meantime the Princess waited for the serpent. Darkness had fallen early, and for some time only the stars could be seen in the clear sky. Then slowly the wonderful winter moon rose into the heavens. At that very moment the King of the Waters raised his head from the pool and darted toward his bride.

"The lobola is paid!" he cried. "Come, let us be off together!"

Then Timba arose, and the serpent lifted her onto his back. She placed her arms around his neck and together they swam down the river, under the light of the great white moon. They passed the silent kraals and the empty fields, and then they came to wide silvery plains stretching out as far as the eye could see. The river flowed on without a sound, and in all that time the King of the Waters neither spoke nor even turned his head.

As the dawn appeared, they reached the borders of a forest, where the bush was so thick that no one could hope to pierce it. The great serpent then brought his bride to the river bank and set her down gently.

"Now remember what you have promised," he reminded her. "You must never be afraid."

Then he disappeared without another word. All that day Timba waited alone, and as night approached there was still no sign of her King. Shuddering, she listened to the cries of wild beasts in search of prey, for she knew that there were wolves and lions close by. Fortunately, nothing bothered her and at dawn all of the strange sounds ceased. Now it was another day and she was still alone, thinking with terror of the approaching night. It was with enormous relief then that at moonrise she saw her bridegroom appear to her once again.

For the second time he took the Princess on his back and they swam down the river, the dark forest on either side. Journeying thus in silence, many hours passed, but at dawn they were still in the heart of the forest. The trees were the tallest that Timba had ever seen, and great festoons of creepers hung from their boughs. Then, unannounced, just as the sun was rising, the river opened out into a wide, still pool, surrounded by walls of dazzling white. Banks of glittering sand shone at the shore, and in every nook and cranny grew the loveliest of ferns, their wide shady fronds lining the water's edge. As if this was not enough, a host of green lily pads pushed out from the shore to frame the center of the pool. Its water lay clear and placid as a mirror, reflecting the dazzling blue of the winter sky. Timba held her breath, for she had never witnessed such beauty before and she longed to alight and rest among the ferns in the bright sunshine. But the King did not linger; he swam forward to the center of the pool. There one could see to the very depths of the water, for the pool was like the clearest crystal, right down to its sandy bottom.

"Follow me," the serpent directed Timba. He paused in

the center of the pool, and then immediately glided under the water with the Princess following right behind. Opening her eyes, she found that they were far below in the depths of the water where the light was rather dim and at first she could see nothing but the waving stems of the water lilies. But she soon discovered that she was standing in front of a group of most beautiful huts. The King led her to the largest one, bidding her enter, and inside, strangely enough, it was quite dry and comfortable. Even more remarkable was the fact that the pretty things she and her sisters had brought to the riverbank were already in the hut; each in its proper place.

Timba was very hungry by now and longed to ask for food, but she dared not say a thing. As if he understood, the great serpent spoke before he left: "Food will appear whenever you should desire it. I will return in the evening. Shut the door, but leave a little hole in the side of the hut, large enough for me to creep through."

And just as her bridegroom had promised, Timba found a delicious meal all ready to eat in the beautiful little pots. It tasted good after the long night's journey; but once she had eaten, there was nothing else to do, and she became bored and lonely. The day passed slowly and as night drew near, it became darker and colder. She lit a fire and shut the door, but remembered to leave a little opening as she had promised. Then she lay down to rest, tired and puzzled by her bridegroom's strange behavior. She was just falling asleep when she heard a snake's scales rustling against the outside of the hut, and for the first time, Timba felt fear. Sitting up she saw his head appear at the little hole, his eyes flickering in the light of the dying fire. He entered and glided toward her. First he touched her feet, then her knees, and then passed right over her head, in absolute silence. Having done this, he turned around and slithered out through the same opening in the hut.

The next day the Princess was alone again; and when at nightfall she tried to sleep, she found that sleep was impossible. For hours she lay awake, tending the fire and

watching the dark hole in the wall. Close to midnight she heard the rustling of the reeds outside, and she began to tremble; but she forced herself to lie quite still and not to utter a sound. The serpent entered as before, laid his head on her feet and her knees, and again glided over her; then he left the hut without a word.

After the serpent had departed, the Princess breathed freely once more, and she tried to relax so that sleep would overtake her. The next morning found her still alone, but as the day edged toward evening she became more troubled and upset.

"Must I spend the rest of my days here?" she asked herself. "Must I always live in this cold dark place, far away from the warmth of the sun? Surely I shall die here before seeing my sisters again." And with this she began to think of her former life. She remembered the many times that she had met her lover among the tall lilies and of all the kindnesses he had shown her.

"No," she cautioned herself. "I must not despair. He will do me no harm; I must keep my promise and not become fearful."

As night fell, once again she lay down in the hut by the wood fire and gazed at the opening in the wall. Hour after hour she remained, listening for the familiar rustling sound; but it did not come. Finally her head began to ache and she was almost sick with fear; sleep was impossible.

Starting up she threw her last bundle of sticks on the little fire to lessen the cold, and she prayed that the dawn would come soon. The flames leaped up for the last time, and at that very moment a faint sound could be heard outside the hut. The King of the Waters had just arrived, and as he entered the hut, his huge flat head was held erect and his eyes were aflame. Timba came very close to screaming, but she clenched her fists to keep herself quiet. The serpent did as he always did, touching her feet, then her knees and last of all her head. Then he glided through the hole into the darkness.

Closing her eyes, the Princess lay back exhausted. As she did, a light breeze caressed her face and she looked up to see what it might be. To her amazement she found that she was no longer in the hut at the bottom of the pool! Somehow she had been brought to the world above, and before her stretched the enchanted pool, radiant and dazzling in the early morning sun.

Her eyes searched everywhere for the serpent, but he had vanished entirely, and was nowhere to be seen. Instead she was surprised to see a magnificent man, strikingly handsome, standing on the bank of the pool. A man in the prime of his life, very powerful and so tall that she had to crane her head far back to study him. Glossy leopard skins hung from his broad black shoulders and round his waist were jackal skins fringed with the tails of the mountain cat. On his arms and at his knees were bracelets of white oxtails, and in his hand he held a great staff that was beautifully carved. This was a very great Chief indeed, and his handsome appearance left Timba speechless. However, one thing did seem familiar to her: his eyes, which were very bright and piercing.

31

The Princess continued to gaze at him in wonderment. He smiled at her.

"You are astonished, and I can well understand," he said. "Yes, I am the serpent, the great King of the Waters. Many years ago my human form was removed by a wicked magician. This magician belonged to a King who hated my father and wished to cause him grief. Knowing of my father's love for me, he turned me into a serpent and decreed that my only kingdom would be in the waters. I could never become a man again until I should find a bride who would not fear me.

"At last I met you, dearest Timba, and now once again, I am a man. Sadly, my father has long been dead and my name is forgotten, so we must seek men and cattle and make a new kingdom for ourselves. My staff will help us, for it has magic powers and I have only to hold it firmly to be victorious over the most powerful enemy. Let us rest here for a while and then we shall go forth together to seek our good fortune."

And that is how the Princess Timba reaped a mighty reward for being courageous. She became a great Queen, both loved and renowned throughout her kingdom, and she lived in great happiness with her beloved King.

The Fairy Frog

A SWAZI TALE

Tombi-Ende was the most beautiful of all the maidens in her father's kingdom. Her eyes were as brown as the eyes of the doe, and when she led the dance her feet were as quick as the feet of the gazelle. Her name, Tombi-Ende, meant "Tall Maiden," and she was indeed taller than any of her sisters. She carried her head high, like a true Princess, and her parents looked upon her with joy and pride. They expected that one day she would be a mighty Queen.

But no one has an altogether happy lot. It is true that Tombi-Ende was tall and beautiful, and that she had the gayest and most wonderful handkerchiefs with which to deck herself, and more beads and bracelets than any other girl in the countryside. But she also had sisters who were not so tall or so beautiful or so greatly admired, and who grew more jealous of her daily. At last, this jealousy grew so intense that it made them quite forget their love for her, and they decided that Tombi-Ende must disappear or no one would ever notice them at all.

And so the jealous sisters worked out a plan to rid themselves of Tombi-Ende. One day they went to her and said, "Come with us. Let us go to the great pit to dig up red ochre, for there is none to be had in the kraal." So every maiden shouldered her pick, and they all walked together, singing and laughing, for many miles. At last they reached a great red pit, many feet deep, surrounded by tall grass on every side. There they stopped; and each girl leaped down in turn to dig out a lump of the precious red earth, and then jumped up again. But when it came time for Tombi-Ende to jump down, the others did not let her jump up again. Instead, each of the jealous sisters threw picks full of earth upon her, until the poor maiden was buried alive. This done, they ran back to their village, leaving their sister behind.

When they arrived home, they told their father that Tombi-Ende had accidentally fallen into the pit and before they could help her to escape, she had suffocated before their eyes. But unfortunately for the girls, each sister told the story in a different way, and the King doubted their innocence in the matter. Ordering his servants to lock all of them into a hut, the King began to mourn for his favorite daughter, for Tombi-Ende the Tall Maiden.

Surprisingly enough, Tombi-Ende was not dead. Although the red earth was very heavy, she was able to breathe through the breaks in the great mound of red ochre that lay above her. And she began to cry out:

"I am Tombi-Ende,
I am not dead,
I am alive like one of you."

For many hours she lay in the red ochre pit, chanting the same call, though fearing more and more that she would never be rescued. When evening came, however, she thought she heard a croaking sound. And indeed she did for at the edge of the pit stood an enormous frog.

"Beautiful Princess," he croaked, "what has befallen you?"

Hearing this question, the lovely maiden cried out in reply, "Alas! My sisters are jealous of me and hate me, and they have thrown earth upon me and left me here, hoping that I would never get out."

"Do not grieve," said the frog, "I will help you." And with that, he jumped into the pit, tunneled through the earth to the Princess, opened his big mouth, and swallowed the Princess in one gulp. Then he jumped up out of the pit, landing directly on the path above, with the Princess safely inside of him.

From there the frog set out upon a long journey. He hopped all night, taking care to avoid any kraals along the way, for the people believed frogs to be an omen of bad luck and he would not have been welcomed. Whenever he passed a bird he sang out:

> *"Do not swallow me,*
> *I carry the Princess Tombi-Ende."*

And no creature touched him. Though the next morning, they very narrowly escaped a great danger, for they came upon a horrible ogress. This Imbula had heard that Tombi-Ende was still alive and had gone in search of her, but when she arrived at the red ochre pit, she had found it empty. Now she was looking for the Princess everywhere, dashing about in a frenzied state, but luckily she paid no attention to the big frog.

At midday the frog stopped hopping. He opened his large mouth, allowing the Princess to step out.

"Wait here and rest," said the frog, "and then we will go on." He croaked three times, and delicious porridge appeared in a little brown pot, all ready for the Princess to eat.

Tombi-Ende ate and soon fell asleep under the bushes, for she was very tired. When evening came, the frog swallowed her once more and they continued on their journey. They had decided not to go to her father's kraal, for fear of her jealous sisters, but rather to go to the home of her grandmother, where Tombi-Ende was sure of every welcome. The frog hopped all through the night, and when morning came he arrived at the grandmother's kraal. Hopping up to the chief hut, the frog sang out loudly:

"I am carrying Tombi-Ende,
The beautiful Princess
Whom they buried in the red pit."

Out came the old grandmother, crying out, "Who is speaking? Who knows what has become of my darling Tombi-Ende?"

"It is I that know all about her," replied the frog. "Bring clean mats to spread before me, and you will see." All the women hurried to get fine new mats, and these they placed before the frog. When this was done, the frog croaked loudly; and opening his mouth as large as before, he allowed the Princess to come out. The women almost fainted as they saw Tombi-Ende standing before them, as tall and beautiful as ever. But their surprise soon turned to joy and there was not one among them who could hear the Princess tell her tale often enough, or sing often enough the praises of the wonderful frog.

"What can we do to reward your kindness?" the grandmother asked of the frog. "There must be something that we can give you."

The frog thought for a moment. "I will only ask you to kill two oxen and two bulls," he said, "and to lay a feast before me."

So a great feast was held, and the frog sat by the Princess's side and was given great honor. He seemed very pleased by the many preparations that had been made in his behalf. The next morning, however, the frog had disappeared, and although the Princess searched for him throughout the kraal, he could not be found.

In the meantime the grandmother had sent a messenger to the King, telling him of his daughter's safety. Upon hearing that all was well, the King was beside himself with joy. First, he released the jealous sisters from their prison, instructing them to prepare robes of state for Tombi-Ende. Then he dispatched his favorite son to bring the Princess home.

The boy arrived, rested a few days at the grandmother's kraal, and then the two set out for home. Great heat and dry earth were their companions on the journey, for the rains had been meager that year and the streams had dried up. The sun was very hot and after hours of walking, the Princess and her brother became very thirsty. Even the underground springs could not be found, for the earth was harder than brick that is dried in an oven, and the water courses were dry. After a time they began to feel faint from the intense heat.

Suddenly, as if in a dream, they saw a strange man standing right across their path. Except for his large size, he appeared to be like other men, and they greeted him with thanksgiving.

"What do you want?" he asked them in a voice that surprised them, for it was of the deepest bass and it rumbled like thunder.

"We are looking for water," said the Prince. "We find that all of the springs are dried up, and we are still many days from home."

"If I should give you water," bargained the giant,

"what will you give me in return?"

"You may ask for anything in my father's kingdom," the Prince answered without thinking.

"I will take this beautiful Princess," said the giant, with a wicked smile playing on his lips. "If you do not give me what I ask for, you will die of thirst. All of the springs are dry within the next three days' journey."

The trials of the past were nothing to the grief and unhappiness that Tombi-Ende and her brother now suffered. What were they to do? To grant the stranger's request might prove fatal for the Princess, but a further lack of water would leave them both helpless. The only solution was to accept the giant's offer and to pray that he would treat them with mercy.

When they agreed to the giant's terms, he chuckled for a few minutes and then led the way to a great fig tree by the side of a dry water course. As he struck his stick upon the ground, a fountain sprang from the very roots of the tree, and its water was as clear as the moon and as cool as the depths of the forest. The brother and sister plunged themselves into the water, allowing it to bathe their faces while they drank of it eagerly and long.

After some time, Tombi-Ende lifted her head, and as her eyes met with the giant, she let out a shriek, for the giant had turned into a most horrible Inzimu. He was monstrous and misshapen, covered with red hair. Behind him on the grass, lay his long tail, and his white pointed teeth forced his thick lips to remain open.

Frightened by his sister's screams, the Prince looked up.

Seeing the monstrous Inzimu, he realized at once just how dangerous their situation was. The ogre was very powerful, and no fighting could possibly save them. He just kept glaring at them, through tiny eyes that radiated evil pleasure.

For Tombi-Ende and her brother, the end seemed to have come; but suddenly there was a loud croak, and out of the fountain sprang the great frog.

"Save me!" cried Tombi-Ende. "Oh help us, frog! No one is as clever and as wise as you!"

The large frog hopped right up to the ogre. The ogre looked down at the frog with disdain and laughed at him with disbelief. The frog allowed the ogre to laugh in this way for a few minutes and then, opening his mouth as large as he could, he swallowed the ogre up, tail and all. At once the frog jumped back into the fountain, and there he remained until the ogre was drowned. Then he returned to Tombi-Ende.

"Ah, my frog, how can I thank you enough?" asked the Princess. "This time you must not disappear. You must come home with us, to be honored as is your due."

And so in three days, Tombi-Ende, her brother, and the frog reached the kraal of the King. As they arrived, they were greeted by the King's guard; beautifully arrayed in otter skins and holding shields and assegais. At their head stood the King, who hailed his two children with joy and affection.

"But why," he inquired, "is that horrible frog at your side? I cannot bear to look at him; let us have him killed."

"Oh no, father," gasped Tombi-Ende, "do not kill him, for he is the best of creatures; twice he saved my life. If it were not for this frog, you would see your Tombi-Ende no more."

As she spoke these words, the frog suddenly turned into the handsomest of men, taller even than Tombi-Ende herself. He was dressed in a splendid array of skins and white ostrich plumes, and everyone could see that he was a Prince. Loud, happy shouts greeted him; but the Princess, herself, did not seem too surprised to see what had happened.

"I am no frog," said the Prince. "My father is a great Chief. The ogre, from whom I rescued the Princess, bewitched me in days gone by. But now that I have won the heart of a maiden, I am free once more. Please, sir, give me the hand of your beloved daughter in marriage, and one hundred cattle shall be yours."

And so a few days later, Tombi-Ende married the fairy frog, an end to the story that brought joy to them both. As for the wicked sisters, the King forgave them, and Tombi-Ende soon forgot all they had done and thought only of her happiness in her new home.

The Enchanted Buck

A SWAZI TALE

LUNGILE SAT WARMING HERSELF in the sunshine, watching her mother put the finishing stitches in her sedwaba. It was a great occasion for her, the most important one in her life.

The sedwaba is the name given by the Kafir people to the full skirt of black oxskins that no maiden wears until her bridal morning. It takes a long time to make, and Lungile's father had prepared the skins many months before. After he had dyed them as black as a dark night with charcoal, Lungile's mother had taken over. She had cut the skins so they fit tightly around the waist, but fell cunningly into folds at the knee, and then she stitched all of the pieces together most beautifully. Now the skirt was ready, and Lungile could set out for the home of her betrothed as soon as she pleased.

Among the Kafirs, the day of the bride's departure is kept a secret from her parents. In that way the bride can slip away without endless farewells. And so when Lungile met with the maidens who were to accompany her to the wedding, the day of departure was arranged amid great secrecy.

It came two days later; and at the first hint of day, Lungile and her maidens set forth on their journey. It was early summer; the first rains were over and the hills were covered with thousands of flowers, vivid scarlet, sky blue and delicate yellow. The air was fresh and clear, and the girls laughed happily and sang songs of travel.

But Lungile was the most joyous of all the maidens, for her bridegroom was a Chief's son; she had chosen him from countless suitors. Many men had flocked to seek her hand, for not only was she beautiful, but also as good and industrious as she was lovely. All of her father's lands had seen her hoe, and the beer that she could make was the best for many miles around. There was no kraal that would not have welcomed her.

For some days the girls journeyed along, and at last they approached the bridegroom's lands. They went directly to his father, the Chief, who greeted them with every kindness, bringing them to a beautiful hut where they were to stay until all of the preparations for the wedding were completed.

Once the bridal party had arrived, every man and

woman in the kraal had something to attend to. While the women ground the corn or went out to gather wood, the bridegroom and his father were busy deciding which oxen should be killed for the feast.

"Let us take two of the oxen that Chief Maginde sent as your sister's wedding present," offered the father. "They are the finest in my herd, but since you are my eldest son, you deserve the best I can give you." And so the oxen were led forth and killed with great ceremony; the bride was delighted that her father-in-law had presented such fine beasts for her pleasure.

All of the women in the kraal fetched the water and prepared the fires for the cooking; only Lungile and her maidens were still. They sat in their hut, thinking of the wedding, which was now approaching quickly. Soon all was ready for the feast and several guests could already be seen nearing the kraal.

The meat was being cut into long strips and then set on the fire to roast. But as the first pieces were being cooked, to the horror of the bridegroom's mother, the meat began to jump about on the fire. She could simply not get them to stay in one place, and after several attempts to make them lie still had failed, she became frightened.

"There must be witchcraft here," she said, and she called her husband to witness the strange sight. But when he arrived with the wedding party, not a trace of the meat remained. It had all disappeared; where, nobody knew.

"The animal was undoubtedly bewitched," proclaimed the Chief. This announcement did not bring joy to the bride's party. She was a stranger, and the people of the kraal might suspect that all was not well with her.

"Bring in the white bull," commanded the Chief. "He is the finest one we have; perhaps if we kill him, we will break the spell."

So the white bull was brought forth. He was the best of all the cattle that the bridegroom's father had received on his daughter's marriage two years before, and because of his color he was held to be an omen of peace and good fortune. He was snow-white from head to tail, except for two long black horns, which gave accent to his beauty. The Chief's kindness and genorosity were praised by all as he prepared to sacrifice this great beast; for everyone felt that now all would go well.

Several of the younger tribesmen were called upon to kill the prize bull. This they did quickly, and then proceeded to place the cut up meat into large pots to boil. Everyone stood by watching intently; especially the bride, who waited anxiously to see what would happen next. There was a deep fear in her heart, for she knew that witchcraft at her wedding meant misfortune would follow.

At the beginning everything seemed quiet. Then the pot of water containing the bull's head began to boil, and at that instant there leaped out of the pot a beautiful young man with the bearing of a great Chief. With incredible speed he raced forward, and even as he did, he changed into a handsome buck with polished horns. Another moment and he was out of sight.

This left the whole bridal party in a great state of

horror. "Bring the bride here!" commanded the Chief. "Without any doubt she is a witch, and it is she who has brought trouble upon us all." Lungile and her weeping maidens stepped forward, all trembling in fright.

"Go back home," shouted the Chief, "and never let us see your face again. You are no wife for my son, or for any decent person, for that matter. I am sending you back to your father, and I am demanding that my marriage gift be returned at once; I leave him to do with you as he sees fit."

"Please, I am innocent of all evil," cried Lungile, protesting her fate. "I have cast no spells, nor do I wish to cause harm to anyone. I will be a good daughter and work hard for you."

But the women of the kraal had banded together and were now screaming, "Go back to your father. You have brought witchcraft here and you are accursed." Then the entire tribe drove Lungile out of their land, and she did not dare to protest her innocence again lest they do her bodily harm.

When Lungile reached her own land, her father and mother received her kindly, and they were horrified to hear of her treatment. They did not for one moment believe that their daughter was a witch; but what could they do to prove otherwise? The marriage gift was returned, and Lungile took her former place in the kraal, working as hard and as well as before. The only difference was that no suitors appeared to ask for her hand, for all had heard the story of the white ox with the black horns and were frightened away. It began to look as if Lungile might never wear the skirt of black oxskins.

Time passed slowly, but nevertheless more than a year went by. Lungile gradually forgot her troubles and the bridegroom that was to have been. It was the time of autumn, and although the air was cool, the sun continued to shine brightly over the great plains. On such a day Lungile went out to gather dried mealie stalks from her father's lands, singing gaily as she walked along the narrow path to the field. Just as she was about to turn into the field, a beautiful buck came into sight. To her great surprise it did not run away, but instead circled her, slipping in and out of bushes. As she stood watching it, it seemed familiar to her.

"Where have I seen this beautiful animal before?" she asked out loud. Then in a single moment she remembered. "Why, it is the very same buck that jumped out of the pot at my wedding feast!"

That memory made her very sad, but she shook off the sadness as she threw back her head and laughed. "Now he shall really be killed; it is many days since we have had meat. I will try to catch him when he passes again."

Playfully the buck continued to circle her, coming closer and closer, but always just slipping from her fingers. Once she even managed to touch him, but he pulled away. Lungile followed after him as he circled ahead, her father's lands fading behind her and the mountains drawing closer. Soon they had come to a stream that led down into a green valley. When they came to the bottom of the valley, Lungile saw a great bush covered with heart-shaped leaves on which a few scarlet blossoms still lingered. The deer stooped down and drank from the stream, and at this instant Lungile jumped forward and seized him by the horns.

To her amazement the buck did not seem to mind that she held him, but instead shook his head and indicated that she should follow him. Up a tiny path he led her, up the valley, always following the course of the stream. Lungile suddenly realized that the animal was so strong that she could not turn back even though she might want to. And in the meantime she had not come upon one person who might help her kill the buck.

The valley was empty and wild, and it was closed at one end by a great round mountain on whose lower slopes reposed a great forest. A blue shadow had begun to creep across the valley, and Lungile saw it and thought, "There is not a soul here and I shall hardly be able to reach home before dark. The buck is much too strong for me; I must let go of him before he leads me to harm."

Sighing as she gave him up, she turned and hurried back, so as to reach the plains again before sundown. Halfway home, out of curiosity she turned her head to see if the buck still remained. To her surprise she learned that the buck had been following her all along. She stood still and in a few minutes the animal was at her side.

"What do you want of me?" asked Lungile.

The buck only looked at her with his great brown eyes and said nothing. Lungile questioned him again. She felt certain by now that the animal was in trouble, and she was beginning to wish that she could help him.

In a soft, low voice the buck answered her this time, "Follow me to yonder forest."

"Yes, I will come with you," agreed Lungile, and she turned once more to the great mountain with the forest at its foot.

Before long they reached the first of the great trees, and there at the very entrance to the forest they saw something that made Lungile cry out in terror. It was a gigantic ogre,

and across his forehead lay a string that held the eyes of many animals. He was seated on the back of a famished looking wolf. This was so terrifying a sight, it can hardly be described.

Lungile turned to run, but the buck gently reassured her, "Trust me. Come and you will see that I can protect you." And he started walking straight toward the ogre. Slowly the girl followed, but she could not keep from shivering when she heard the ogre call out to the buck, "Ha, you will do splendidly for my friend the wolf's

supper, and that fine young girl will be perfect for mine."

Opening his huge mouth even wider, the ogre stretched out his long arms and darted forth to catch the buck. To Lungile's distress, the buck did not resist him; but at the moment the arms of the ogre touched him, the buck was in an instant changed into a handsome young man. The wolf, terrified at this display of magic power, ran trembling into the bush; the ogre, unprepared for the wolf's action, was killed by low branches as the wolf rushed forward.

The young man ran to the body of the dead ogre and removed the crown of animal's eyes from the monster's head. Having done this, he threw the eyes upon the ground. Instantly they became living deer, all looking toward the young man, their eyes filled with love.

Turning to Lungile, who was now at his side, the young man spoke, "Be kind to these animals and help them. Always remember that I too was once a buck. Please stay here for a few days and do something for me. Every morning gather fresh spinach and sing this fairy song:

"Once my true love was a buck,
Once my true love was a buck;

Now he is changed into a fine, strong, young man.
Now, bucks . . . Oh, bucks,
Change yourselves and become young men."

"I will do as you say," promised Lungile with love and

admiration shining from her eyes. "But first tell me two things; are you not the white bull who was killed at my wedding feast? And who are these deer who are to be transformed?"

"I am indeed that very same white bull," replied the young man. "I was a great Chief, and because my lands were better than Chief Maginde's and my cattle finer and my people stronger, he hated me. One day he managed to bewitch me and turn me into a white bull; all of my people he made into deer. There was no escape from this enchantment until I could change my shape and become a man once again. Chief Maginde sent me in the form of the white bull as a marriage gift to the father of your bridegroom, and that is how I came to be there. It is because of me that you lost your betrothed, but please do not grieve for him. Now that I am once again a great Chief, I can give you everything you could possibly want and all of my love, if you will be my bride."

Lungile was filled with great joy and agreed to accept his offer, for the fairy buck was handsomer and more gallant than any youth she had ever beheld. She remained in the forest for many days, just as her young man had instructed her to. Every morning at sunrise, when the dew was still heavy, she arose and sang the fairy song as she gathered the spinach up and down the hillside. And every day more and more of the deer came from the mountains and assembled in the forest. They brought with them their little ones and in seven days, many thousands of them had gathered together. On the seventh morning as she sang the magic song, all of the bucks and the does and the little ones began to change form, and by sunrise they were men, women and children.

Thus the enchanted buck regained his people and at the same time won for them a most kind and beautiful Queen. He took Lungile back to her father, whom he presented with a marriage gift such as no one had ever seen before. After that he made Lungile his wife, amid the greatest of rejoicing ever known in that land.

The Beauty &
The Beast
A SWAZI TALE

M ANY YEARS AGO, there lived a very pretty girl whose name was Mulha. Her name meant the "Fair One," and indeed she was very fair to behold.

Mulha lived with her father and mother and two little sisters in a home that was surrounded by mountains. Because the land was so poor, few other people had settled there, and the family was often lonely. Their land was so poor that Mulha's mother was obliged to grow all her crops in a fertile valley some miles away, and quite often she was gone for many days. She would take her hoe and set off, leaving Mulha in charge of the kraal.

Once when the time of planting arrived, Mulha's father was away, on a hunting expedition. Since he was not expected back for some days, his wife knew that she would have to leave her three children alone. As Mulha was almost fully grown, the mother put her in charge of the others.

The mother made sure that plenty of corn and many kinds of beans were available for the girls to prepare for their meals. Then before leaving, she called them over to the big pot that stood on one side of the hut.

"Children," she began, "never open this pot. You have plenty to eat, and you will need nothing else. Promise me faithfully that you will obey. If you are good, I will give you all a little feast when I return; we will kill a goat and make beer, and have a merry time."

The children promised to obey their mother and not to touch the pot; so the mother bade them farewell and started on her journey. For a few days the girls were quite happy. They cooked their food and kept house and not for some time had the kraal looked so neat and tidy. But then they grew weary of being alone, and the two younger children said to their sister, "We are tired; our mother stays away too long."

Upon hearing this, Mulha told them, "Do you know what I am going to do?"

"No," they answered.

"I am going to open the big pot."

"Oh, no, Mulha, you musn't!" said the other two, their voices quivering. "We all promised faithfully that we would not touch it."

"I want to see what is inside," said Mulha with great

56

determination. And with that she went straight to the pot and opened it; but instead of the food that she expected to see, out came a huge ogre whose body filled the entire hut. There was no room left for anyone else, and the three girls fled in terror. But the ogre called after them in such sweet tones that he overcame their fears and convinced them to return.

"I will do you no harm," said he; "you two older girls can go out to fetch the water while I keep your youngest sister here to cook the food." They did as he told them, but while the two were away, he placed the youngest girl in the pot to be cooked for dinner. When they returned, they found that the pot was already warm, although they could see no fire. "Come," said the ogre, "and sit down. I have a nice little dish ready for you that your little sister helped me to prepare."

But just at that moment a huge bee flew in at the door and buzzed all around the sisters' ears. The buzzing became words and the girls understood them to say, "Do not eat anything! It is your own little sister who has been put in the pot in your absence. You must free her before she comes to great harm at the hands of the ogre."

The two girls told the monster at once that they were not hungry, and they sat very still trying to think of a way to rescue their youngest sister. But no sooner had they thought of an idea that seemed good, than the ogre seemed to sense it. It was almost impossible to escape from the huge monster, who seemed to be everywhere and know everything.

Finally as the darkness of night reached its blackest time, Mulha in a final desperate attempt to escape ran from the hut without warning. The terrible ogre followed close behind her as she plunged down the path. No sooner had Mulha run from the hut, than the other sister leaped toward the pot. Snatching off the lid, she pulled her youngest sister up from the swirling water. By carrying and dragging her, she managed to reach the door of the hut; and from there they moved toward a thick, tangled clump of bushes. Here they paused just long enough for the little one to regain her strength, and then slipping through the bushes they ran toward the river. Swimming down the stream, the two girls reached the bottom of the valley just at the moment of dawn.

Making their way to the fields in which their mother worked, they told her their terrible story and pleaded with her to come and help Mulha. But the mother shook her head sadly. "This is what comes," she said, "of disobedience. I can do nothing until the proper time; we must wait for your father."

In the meantime the ogre had discovered that the two younger sisters had escaped, and his wrath and anger could hardly be contained in the hut. Mulha feared that he would seize her for his next meal, but luckily he kept her alive, not wanting to use up his last source of food.

It was not long, however, before the wicked Inzimu became hungry again, and not ready yet to eat Mulha he left her alone in the hut while he went out to search for fresh prey. This was just the opportunity that Mulha had been waiting for, and she set out at once. Running down winding paths and always following the course of the river, she finally managed to reach her mother's lands. There at last she found both her mother and her sisters and they embraced each other joyfully.

But escape was not enough for Mulha. She wanted to seek revenge on the monster for all the grief he had caused her to suffer, and she begged her mother to kill him. Once more her mother shook her head and said, "What can we do? Your father is not back yet." No sooner had these words left her lips than their father came into sight. After embracing him, they told him their story, and so great was his anger and indignation that he seized his shield and assegais and went forth to find the monster and kill him.

On the next day he came back looking sad and tired. "We cannot return to our home again," he said to his wife. "We must build a new hut here. I threw my assegais at the monster with all possible force and skill, but they all fell to the ground, powerless. It is senseless to think of revenging ourselves; the monster is a magician."

Upon hearing this, the mother was worried. She called her three girls and told them what had happened. The Inzimu was not dead, so it would not be safe for them to return to their home. But more than that, the ogre would be searching for them and especially for Mulha, who was the last to escape. To make sure that Mulha would not be harmed, her parents decided to send her away.

"You shall go to your married sister," the mother said. "She is in a good position and will look after you; and very soon, no doubt, someone will want you for his wife. But remember, Mulha, go straight along the road and make sure that you do not touch the manumbela that grows by the wayside."

For the journey her sisters dressed Mulha in a piece of black cloth, gaily striped with green and blue, which they knotted around her waist. Mulha put on her brightest beads; and as she left, she knew that no girl in all of Swaziland was prettier or walked with a lighter step. Her family watched her go with a feeling of pride, and they had little doubt that she would soon marry the son of a Chief.

Mulha set out planning to be very careful and obedient to her mother's words. She remembered well the grief her last sad experience had brought. And for a long time she did just as she had been told. But it was the time of full summer and, the afternoon was very hot, so she soon became very thirsty. There was no water in sight but as she turned a bend in the road, she saw a beautiful manumbela tree covered with rich ripe berries. The manumbela, as you may not know, is the Forbidden Fruit.

Mulha looked at it longingly; and the more she looked at the berries, the more she longed to have some. At last she could resist no longer, and she climbed straight up the tree to get the fruit that was forbidden. No sooner had she reached the top of the tree and picked the first of the luscious looking berries than a deep bass voice called out of the tree trunk, "Dear good girl, please give me some

fruit." The voice was so deep that as it spoke, the whole tree shook.

Mulha gathered some more of the fruits and made her way down the tree, feeling uneasy and frightened. As she reached the bottom, the trunk of the tree opened and out came a great Ogress, an Imbula, with an ugly snout like a wolf's and with red hair covering her entire body. The ogress took the fruit and swallowed it greedily. Then she said to Mulha, "You are not safe traveling alone, a pretty girl like you. Give me all of your things and I will give you mine and then you will not be so attractive to everyone that you may meet on your way. In that way your journey will be much safer for you."

This seemed to make sense to Mulha. So she gave the Ogress the striped cottons that she had worn so proudly. She did not want to part with her beautiful beads, but the Imbula insisted on having them and promised that she would give everything back when they approached the married sister's kraal. She then gave Mulha her own skin to wear as a disguise.

To Mulha's horror, she found that the skin clung to her as tightly as if it were her own. Nothing could remove it. The Imbula, on the other hand, looked like a pretty girl. Her horrid lumpy skin with its red hair and her wolf's snout had disappeared altogether. It was the Ogress who was now "Mulha, the Fair One", while the real beauty had become the loathsome monster.

As they approached her sister's kraal, Mulha asked the Ogress to give back her dress and ornaments, but to her horror, the monster absolutely refused. When they came to the gate, it was the Imbula who went right in to ask for her sister, and she was welcomed by all and given great honor.

"What are we to do with your companion?" asked the married sister, eyeing Mulha with a look of disgust.

"Oh, just put her anywhere," said the Imbula. "She can stay and eat with the dogs in some old hut."

"Very well," agreed the married sister. "She can live with one of the old women where she will not be seen or trouble anyone."

And so, the Ogress was able to pass as a beautiful maiden and to command great attention from all. She did after all look like a very pretty girl, except for one thing. All Imbulas have a tail, just as Inzimus do, and it is impossible for them to get rid of this. The Ogress had managed to wind hers round and round her waist, and there it remained, hidden underneath her clothing. Each day she feared that it would be discovered, but no one dreamed of such a possibility. So for a long time all went well for the Imbula.

In the meantime the real beauty, Mulha, lived in a state of disgrace in the hut of an old woman. There she suffered great trials because of the trick the Imbula had played upon her. Only one good thing happened: she discovered that the skin she wore endowed her with magic powers, and so she began to use them.

"Tell me," she asked the old woman, "would you like to be made young again?"

"Yes indeed," replied the old woman licking her dried lips.

"Very well, you shall be," promised Mulha. And the next morning everyone wondered what had happened to the old woman, for once again she looked like a young girl. She did not dare tell the others what had happened, for Mulha had bound her to secrecy, fearing that her magic powers might be destroyed by the real Imbula. So the two of them lived quietly together, but in great comfort, for Mulha had discovered that she could obtain choice food for both of them by commanding it. The scraps that were thrown to them by her sister remained untouched.

In the meantime the real monster was acquiring many many suitors, for the fame of her beauty had spread far and wide. She finally announced her engagement to a very wealthy and handsome Prince. Her behavior, however, was most puzzling, because she would never allow her betrothed as much as one kiss and even declared that she was far too modest to allow him to sit by her side. The real beauty knew the actual reason for the Ogress's actions, but to everyone else, it seemed very strange.

Some time after the engagement was announced, Mulha's sister was down by the river, washing some garments, when she saw Mulha the monster appear. She hid in order to observe what the strange creature intended to do. The supposed monster approached the water, and no sooner had the misshapen being touched the water than her skin floated away and she became the most beautiful

64

maiden that was ever seen. Stretching out her graceful arms, she sang:

> *"Come, maidens, come,*
> *Come and play with me,*
> *Come and play in the water."*

From all sides beautiful maidens appeared, who played and laughed with her as their Princess. After Mulha had been herself for some time, the horrible skin floated back toward her body and once again she became a beast.

The married sister turned toward her home in great consternation. Sensing that something was not right, she consulted an aging Princess who was well known for her wisdom. This person advised that they should both observe what happened the very next time the monster went down to bathe. They did, and beheld the very same thing. Confronting the creature, just as she was about to leave the river, they questioned her repeatedly. She soon told them that she was the true Mulha, and that she had been overcome by an Imbula; but she made it quite clear that she did not wish to change her situation.

"Why do you bother me? I have everything I want, and I do not care to be troubled. You took the Imbula in as your sister; now you can keep her."

"It is not right that men should be deceived by a monster," said her sister. "I will speak to the King about this."

So Mulha's sister and the aging Princess went before the King and set the problem before that mighty person.

He soon devised a clever method of settling the question of which was the true beauty and which the real beast.

"Dig a big hole in the middle of the kraal and place in it all kinds of food and a calabash filled with plenty of fresh milk. Then make every woman in the kraal walk around the hole by herself, and we shall soon see which is the Imbula."

All was prepared as the King commanded, and all the women in the kraal, young and old, were told to walk around the hole. At last it came the turn of the Imbula.

"It is not necessary for me to walk around the hole," she said. "Everyone knows that I am a beautiful maiden. Besides, I am far too shy to show myself off before everybody."

She twisted and turned and spoke in a tiny sweet voice, just as she had done whenever the Prince approached her. But the King would have none of it and commanded her to walk around the hole or suffer death.

So the Imbula was obliged to change her plans and to begin the walk around the hole. At the sight of the fresh white milk, all of her bestial instincts were aroused and she forgot everything else. Without warning her tail uncoiled and slithered down into the hole to suck up the milk; for no Inzimu, male or female, can control its tail when milk is on the ground. This the King had counted on when he laid the trap.

Learning at last who the real monster was, the King signaled his hunters to kill her. It was at the Imbula's moment of death that Mulha regained her own true form.

And so radiantly beautiful was she that the Prince who had been deceived by the Ogress fell in love with her at once. Arrangements were soon made for their wedding, and one hundred cows were paid to Mulha's father. This made him a rich man, and Mulha's happiness was made complete after so many adventures.

The Story of the Shining Princess

A 'MSUTO STORY

FAR UP IN THE MOUNTAINS, nestling in a cool green valley, stood a most beautiful kraal. The hut was a bright green, for it was finely thatched with grass, and the floor within was of the firmest and most brilliantly polished red earth. Around the inner walls stood the cooking pots made of red clay, and along with these were shining green calabashes overflowing with the richest milk and cream. On part of the floor, lay fine green mats, but on another part lay the prettiest one of all, woven of gold-colored grass. Encircling the hut itself was a high green fence, a work of beauty, too; indeed, everything was in perfect order and no other kraal in the countryside could claim to be its equal.

This was the home of a great Chief's wife. The Chief, who had been dead for many years, had left his Queen alone in the world with only one little daughter named Maholia, who was three years old when he died. His Queen had once been a most beautiful woman, and as the little girl grew up, she became just as lovely as her mother. The greatest care was taken in rearing her, and she soon became as good and obedient as she was charming.

The Queen had not married again, for in her tribe this did not befit a King's wife, and so she lived only for the child, Maholia, and they loved one another dearly. Maholia was the envy of every little girl in the country, because everything she wore was the color of the golden moon: her necklaces, her bracelets, and the gold band that she wore around her neck. As she grew up, she became more and more celebrated for her beauty and charm; in fact she was so lovely that she dazzled the eyes of all who beheld her, and she became known among her people as the Shining Princess.

Time went on, and as she grew into womanhood, many, many suitors came forth to ask her hand in marriage. There was not a Chief's son in that part of the country who did not long to make her his wife. But neither the Princess herself nor her mother were enamored of any of the men who presented themselves, and so they waited for the right one to appear.

Then one day, an ambassador, a chief Induna, from a very powerful King arrived in the kraal. He had searched in many places for a beautiful maiden to become the wife of the King's son. But though he had traveled far and wide and brought many girls back to his King's kraal, not one had suited the old Chief. And so the King had sent the chief Induna out yet again, to yet more distant lands, to inspect all the Princesses who were famous for their beauty. Now after many months of traveling, with no success, the Induna had come to see the Shining Princess. He had heard talk of her and thought it wise to seek her out, though he secretly feared that he would meet with disappointment once again.

At the sight of the green kraal, the hopes of the ambassador rose. They soared even higher when the Princess came to the door to greet him, for there she stood, her blackness glistening from head to foot in the bright sunlight. Round her neck were thick bars of red-gold copper. Adorning her shapely arms from wrist to elbow were copper and brass rings, and these appeared also on her slender ankles and reached almost to her knees. A girdle of golden beads encircled her waist, and its long glistening fringes hung over her short apron of skin. Over her pretty shoulders hung her cloak, embroidered in circles of gold and bordered with a wide band of shining beads. Even her snuff-calabash was of gold colored jackalskin. All of her movements were full of grace, and her laughing lips and bright eyes were a sign of the kindness in her heart.

When the Induna saw this beautiful woman, clad in gold and shining like the rising moon, he rejoiced and said, "This is indeed the Princess that I have been searching for! There is no doubt that this is the true wife for our great King's son!"

He begged to see Maholia's mother and formally demanded the hand of her daughter. But many days passed in discussion, since the Queen was not anxious to part with her only child. The Induna, however, spoke so well of his master's power and riches, and so eloquently of the bravery and wisdom of the bridegroom, that at last she consented to the union. The ambassador could now return to his home with the joyous news for his King.

Upon his arrival, the King listened to the description of Maholia and then heaped great praise on the Induna for his selection of such a maiden. While the Induna rested, the King gathered together the marriage gift of cattle for Maholia's mother. This consisted of one hundred beautiful animals, at the head of which marched a fairy ox, a beast who was truly magnificent. He was as black as charcoal, save for two long white horns, and between his shoulders burned a steady light, which illumined his path at night and gave him magic powers. This beast was the King's great pride, but he was considered due payment for so fair a Princess as Maholia.

When all was ready, the wedding party started out to fetch the bride and at the same time to deliver the marriage gift to her mother. The Queen was delighted with the cattle and especially with the fairy ox who led them. Upon receiving him, she took him directly to her daughter. "Here," she said to her child, "take this ox with you. He is my present to you; your journey will be a long one,

71

and you will be happy to ride him when you are tired."

Then turning to the King's men, she warned them, "Do not leave my daughter alone on your return journey. I am afraid of what can happen to her. If you should leave her, I shall know that at once, for the corner of our hut where she always sat will crumble away."

Of course the wedding party promised faithfully to guard Maholia with the greatest care. And feeling reassured, the Princess and her mother parted with both tears of joy and tears of sadness. Thus Maholia and her attending maidens set forth upon their journey with the King's men.

For two days all went well. But on the third day the men came upon hundreds of deer of every kind, and behind these appeared great herds of elephants and giraffes. In short the country was abundant with game, and the King's men were not able to resist such overwhelming temptation. Off they went to hunt, with even the maidens joining the party, all in pursuit of the fleeing animals. Only the Shining Princess stayed behind, with the fairy ox close by her side. At that very moment, as her mother sat in the hut anxiously thinking of her daughter, the corner on which the golden mat had lain, cracked from end to end and crumbled away. And the Queen knew that Maholia was in danger.

In the meantime the wedding party went on with the hunt; and the farther they went, the more animals appeared. The hunters forgot all about the poor bride and continued their chase for many days, while she sat alone.

Finally it was her misfortune to be discovered by a group of cannibals, who seized her with ease and carried her off. Luckily their attempt to capture the fairy ox failed; he managed to escape them with one great leap into the air, and then he flew like the wind to the hut of the Princess's mother.

The poor Queen was there to meet him at the gate of the kraal, for she knew some evil had befallen her daughter. She knelt before the great ox, while he stood and related his tale.

"But where is Maholia now?" cried the Queen. "Where have they taken her?"

"I know nothing else," replied the ox. "As soon as the cannibals took her, I came to you with all possible speed. Please do not despair; all will turn out well!"

In the meantime the King and his son waited and waited for the expected bride. Weeks and months passed by, and they began to fear that some great calamity had overtaken the party. Then, one by one their men straggled in to tell their shameful tale, that they had left the Princess all alone and forgotten all about her. They had finally returned to the place where they had left her, but she was nowhere to be found though they had searched the forest far and wide. The King was furious and had all the men put to death; and then calling his wise men together, he asked them for their advice. How could the Princess be found? The wise men decided that the bridegroom, himself, must go with a group of select men to search for the bride, starting at her mother's home.

The anguished Queen received the party with much joy, but her joy became complete despair when she learned that they knew nothing of her daughter. When they questioned her, she told them of the return of the fairy ox and the story that he had brought her.

"Please, Queen Mother, be of good cheer," begged the Prince. "I, myself, will take the fairy ox and together we will search for your daughter. I promise you that I shall never return until I can bring her back with me."

Having uttered these words, the Prince tarried no longer. Taking the fairy ox, he set forth upon his journey. He traveled for weeks and months, but not one trace of the Princess did he discover, until the day that he came upon a marula tree, covered with shining yellow fruit.

This would be just the fruit to make excellent cider, he thought as he smelled the sweet fragrance of the fruit. I must taste it.

He had eaten but a few berries when a deep voice came out of the tree.

"What do you want?" it demanded to know.

"I am in search of the Shining Princess," retorted the Prince. "Can I be assured that I am following the right course?"

"Keep going forward," advised the marula tree, "until you come to the big fig tree."

And so the Prince journeyed farther, through country overgrown with bush, until he came to an immense tree covered with little red figs. The figs were so numerous that they even grew on the roots, and the leaves were so

thick that no sunlight could pierce them. Sitting down to rest in the tree's deep shade, the Prince said, "I seek the Shining Princess. Am I going the right way?"

"Oh, yes," answered the fig tree, "go on until you come to a big river. Beyond it lies a great forest and in that forest you will find the Princess." The Prince jumped up, filled with renewed hope, and ran along the course of the stream. On the next day he found himself in full view of a deep river; but it was so flooded and swollen, he could not hope to cross it.

"Climb on my back," said the fairy ox, who was the faithful companion of the Prince. "I will carry you across the river."

The Prince was happy to do just that, and the ox plunged into the water, swimming across with no difficulty and then racing over a huge plain beyond. In the far distance the forest was soon visible, and it appeared to grow larger every hour, until finally the two were within its borders. The trees there were taller and thicker than any the Prince had ever seen, and their branches were completely entwined at their peaks. No path at all was visible to the eye, for only the dimmest light filtered through to the forest floor.

The Prince was forced to wander through the thick growth, groping for hours in a land without sun, without one open glade. Then at last, in the distance, he seemed to detect a shining pool of water; and guided only by this distant shimmer, he plunged forward. Drawing nearer, he could see that the pool was surrounded by reeds, the tallest of which stood in the center. The gleam of the water grew brighter and more golden, until at the end, as he burst through the thicket, he found that this was no pool at all, but rather the Shining Princess herself, seated in a circle of tall grasses.

The Prince hailed her with delight and thanksgiving, for never had he hoped to find such a beauty as she. Maholia, on her part, welcomed him warmly and soon told him how she had been taken through this very forest by the cannibals who had captured her. Luckily, she had managed to escape from them one dark night, as they attempted to bring her to their King. And ever since then she had been living in the midst of the great bush. After the Princess had told of her adventures, the Prince had to tell of his, ending his account by telling Maholia how beautiful she was and how she was worth every danger he had encountered. This was her favorite part of his story, and she wanted to hear it over and over again. Thus they sat for hours among the ferns, telling one another of their wanderings and of their love for each other.

Indeed, they might never have left the forest, had not the Princess suddenly remembered her mother and the deep anguish that she must be suffering.

"But how will I be able to get you home?" asked the Prince. "Everyone will envy me such a beautiful woman, and they will try to steal you away from me. If only it were possible to hide you."

"I can help you!" exclaimed the fairy ox, nuzzling the bride affectionately. "I will turn the Princess into an ugly old man for now, and then no one will trouble us."

So for the time being, Maholia became a little old man, and she mounted the fairy ox with her beloved Prince beside her. Together they all flew over forest, river and mountain; and at the end of seven days, they reached the home of Maholia's mother.

Then at last, all was safely ended. For the Shining Princess became a dazzling bride, and she and her husband set out for their own kingdom. There they reigned in great peace and happiness, with the fairy ox remaining as their devoted follower and adviser for the rest of his days.

The Three Little Eggs

A SWAZI TALE

It WAS AN EARLY MORNING in midwinter. The sun was just rising over the great plains in a silver haze, and then melting into a ball of pale gold. As the wide stretches of veld came into the light, they looked burnt dry, for the rains had long been over. The sun had shone every day, all day long, and there was a pleasant heat to be felt in the land. Except for the water courses, the whole country appeared golden, and the few great evergreen trees stood up in vivid contrast to the bleached summer grasses.

By the side of a great fig tree there was a poor little hut surrounded by a woven fence. Near by was a small patch of cultivated ground, where a few dried mealie stalks were still standing. The sun had barely touched the top

79

of the tree, when a woman hurried from the hut and passed through the kraal gate. You could see that she was married, by her full skirt of oxskins and her peaked head-dress. Besides, she carried on her back a dear little baby girl, wrapped in a goatskin and half-asleep, and by her side ran a jolly little boy. The mother, herself, was still young and pretty, though her face was worn and thin and if you looked closely you could see that her arms were covered with scars and burns, as if she had been dealt with badly.

She stood for a few minutes and looked toward the wide plains. Then she turned to where the great hills rose up, ruddy and golden in the early sun. She seemed to hesitate, but only for a time; at last she faced the mountains and entered a tiny pathway that wound its way into a wooded gorge and eventually led hundreds of feet above the plains. She did not sing as she went, but rather cast many frightened glances behind her, as if fearing that she would be seen. No one followed her, however, and as the little hut disappeared from sight, she grew less anxious and walked with a lighter step.

She was running away from her husband. For four years she had been married, and each year he had been more unkind to her. Not only had he demanded a great deal of her, but he had often beat her and scarcely given her or the children enough food to sustain them. She, being good and obedient, had tried hard to please him, but he had only become more and more cruel to her and the children. Two days before, he had gone off to a big dance in a faraway kraal, and the poor woman had so dreaded his return that she had decided to run away and beg her living as best she could. On the other side of the mountain were many kraals, and she was sure that she could find enough work to provide food for the three of them.

As she walked and thought about this, the baby girl awoke and started playing and laughing. They were following the course of a stream, where only a trickle of water remained and the thick bushes stood dry and leafless. As the mother chanced to look up, she saw a fluffy white nest, hanging from a long bough, which was otherwise barren.

"How pretty!" she thought. "That will be the very thing to amuse the baby."

Reaching up to the bough, she lifted the soft nest down, while her young son looked on with great interest. How surprised she was to discover that the nest contained three little eggs, for it was still many months before the spring would appear.

"Hold it carefully," she cautioned her little one, "so that you do not smash the tiny eggs."

The day had passed quickly and now, noticing that the sun was sinking and the air was growing colder, she began to walk more quickly; for they were on the hilltops, where there is a sharp frost every evening. Finally, not seeing a hut in sight, and having no covering except for one poor goatskin, the mother became distressed. "Where shall we rest tonight?" she asked herself. "There is nothing here but open country."

In reply, a tiny voice at her ear said, "Take the road to the right; it will lead you to a safe place."

She turned this way and that, looking for the one that had spoken to her, and discovered to her amazement that the voice belonged to one of the little eggs in the fluffy nest. Heeding its advice, she looked to the right and saw a tiny pathway, which to tell the truth, she had not noticed before. And so she took it at once, just as the sun was disappearing and the white frost was beginning to show. In a matter of minutes she had reached a beautiful hut, under the side of a great rock.

The hut appeared to be abandoned, but it was warm and comfortable within. On the walls hung karosses of oxskin and goatskin, and on the floor there were calabashes overflowing with delicious thick milk. There was food already prepared in little red pots: crushed mealies and monkey-nuts. The little boy and the baby girl cried with delight, and the poor mother was pleased beyond measure.

First the little nest was carefully laid aside, and then both mother and children partook of a sumptuous meal; for needless to say, they were quite hungry. The little boy fell asleep soon after, wrapped in the warm skins, but his sister cried and would not lie quietly. So the mother tied the child on her back once more, and sang the Kafir cradle-song, which is as pretty a song as you will hear. She rocked gently from side to side, in time to the rhythm:

"Tula, mtwana
Binda, mtwana

U nina u fulela
U nina u fulela
 Tula, mtwana."

"Be quiet, my baby;
Be still, my child;

Your mother has gone to get green mealies,
Your sisters are all gone gathering wood,
 So be quiet, baby be still.
Your father has gone a-walking,
He has gone to drink good beer,
Your mother is working with a will,
 So be quiet, baby, be still."

Soon the tiny black head nodded forward, the little round arms relaxed, and the baby girl was fast asleep. The tired mother put her down, and in a few minutes, she too was dreaming by her children's side.

Early the next morning they set forth again, this time feeling refreshed. They continued on the same path, the baby girl carrying the little eggs as she had before. Toward midday, they came to a point where there was a fork in the road. Not knowing which path to take, the woman stood for some time, looking confused. Then another tiny voice, much the same as the first, spoke in her ear. It was the second little egg this time, and it said, "Take the road to the left."

So she started down the left-hand path until she came

to an enormous hut, three times as big as any she had ever seen. Full of curiosity, she went right up to the door, and there she discovered an unforgettable scene. The calabashes and pots within were all blood-red in color, and so thin that the breezes swayed them as if they were large bubbles, for they were as light as the air. One of the big pots was blown right across the room, and as the poor mother's eyes followed its course, she almost screamed aloud; for on the side of the hut where the pot came to rest, a huge monster lay fast asleep. He was most immense, both tall and stout, and his body was covered with brick-red hair. Two horns grew out of his head, and his long tail lay curled across his knees. Without any doubt, he was an Inzimu, an ogre if you will. Fear raced through the mother's body, knowing that the ogre would kill them all, if he should awake and see them.

"What shall I do?" she cried to herself as she rushed away from the door. "I am afraid that we will all be killed!"

It was then that the third little egg spoke up saying, "Do you see that great stone? Lift it and carry it with you to the very top of the hut."

Looking around the woman tried to determine which stone the little egg wanted her to take, for there were many in sight. But her eyes soon focused on one round white stone, the perfect size to drop through the thatched roof. Surely this one would kill whoever it fell on. But how could she lift it up?

84

"However can I pick it up?" pondered the woman. "It seems so very heavy."

"Do as I bid you," repeated the egg.

So the woman stooped down and attempted to raise the stone. To her surprise, she found it light enough to take to the back of the hut with little difficulty. There she was afraid to leave her babies alone on the ground, so she lifted them onto the roof first. Then she climbed up herself, clutching the stone in her hand.

"Now," said the egg, "you are ready to let the stone drop down on top of the monster."

Before dropping the rock, the mother peeped through the thatched roof to determine the exact spot where the ogre lay. She feared that any mistake might be fatal for them all. It was just as she was about to drop the rock, that she realized the door of the hut was opening; and to her horror, a second ogre appeared, dragging several bodies after him.

"Now we shall certainly be found out," said the mother. "All is over." But she managed to keep the children quiet while the second Inzimu prepared his evening meal. He was so engrossed in what he was doing, that he stopped only once to sniff the air.

"There is something tasty hidden in this hut, but I don't know where it is," he muttered to himself.

After finishing his preparations, the Inzimu looked around the hut, but fortunately he never thought of going up on the roof. He ate his dinner with relish and soon fell asleep next to the first Inzimu, while the mother watched in terror from the roof.

"Now there are two Inzimus," she gasped, "I cannot kill both with this one stone. What am I to do now?"

"You had better come down as quietly as you can," whispered all the little eggs at once, "and with your babies run as fast as you possibly can."

They had hardly finished speaking before she began to slip down very quietly, the little boy helping her with his baby sister. Although they were trembling in every limb, they managed to be on their way in the next few minutes. Luckily, the Inzimus did not awaken, and it was not too long before the big hut was out of sight.

The poor mother felt that she could take a deep breath once again. She walked along wishing that she would find a kraal and people that she could talk to. She was thinking of this as she wound in and out of the bushes, which grew thicker and more thorny. Then great trees began to appear and as the path gave a sudden turn, she almost collided with a huge evergreen tree, which seemed to spring up before them. To add to her astonishment, a horrible ogress lay sleeping under the tree. Hard to believe as it was, she was even uglier than the Inzimus, for she had a hideous snout, just like a wolf's, and between her eyes was one little horn. Her snoring was so violent that the very branches of the tree shook unceasingly.

Now the mother was sure that her last hour had truly come, for there seemed to be no means of escape. It was impossible to return to the hut of the Inzimus and she could not go forward, for the bushes were too thick to pass through. But the little eggs brought comfort to her once again.

"Look on your right; a big ax lies there."

She looked and just as the voices said, there lay a great ax, gleaming in the sunlight. It was so large that it must have belonged to the Ogress, but somehow the woman managed to lift it.

"That was good," the little eggs encouraged her. "Now put your little ones into the lower branches of the tree; and then when they are safe, climb up yourself. Creep along the great arm of the tree over the monster's head, and make sure that you hold on to the ax tightly."

Once again the mother did as she was told. She lifted her little son up into the branches and found that he was able to hold his baby sister among the leaves. Then mounting the tree herself, the woman crept forward with the ax in her hand. As she reached the spot directly above the monster's head, she became so frightened that she almost toppled from the tree. Again the little eggs spoke:

"Aim the ax at the monster's head and drop it!"

She did as she was told, and the ax hit the Ogress just above the horn, but to her dismay, the blow did not kill the beast; it merely stunned her.

"Slide down the tree!" urged the third little egg, "and kill the monster before she revives."

In a moment the mother had slid from the tree and was running forward with desperate courage to kill the beast before she herself was the victim.

Finally she met with success; she finished the beast with one mighty blow. As soon as it was over, she stepped back to give thanks for her victory and to rest up from her ordeal. When she was standing several feet away, she glanced back toward the monster that she had slain. And she could hardly believe what she saw with her eyes, for out of the Ogress came an endless procession of men, women and children, as well as cattle and goats. One after another they filed out, spilling onto the already crowded path. There were actually hundreds of creatures, for the Ogress had eaten every form of animal life and whole families of men in her wicked lifetime. When all had been released, there were enough people and animals to start a great kraal. Each one of them approached the young mother to thank her for making their freedom possible. And when all were assembled, their leaders came forward, asking her to honor them by consenting to be their Queen.

"Thank you," she said, "but I must be truthful with you and tell you that I should not have been able to do it without these three little eggs." As she told them this, she turned to show them the little white nest. She had barely touched it with her fingers, when all saw it disappear. And in the place where it had rested, the earth began to tremble. The strange quakes kept up until three handsome princes rose up where the nest had been. The eldest of the three knelt before the woman, and taking her hand, said,

"You, dear woman, have freed us from the spell of a wicked enchantress by being so full of courage. I beg of you to agree to become my wife, in order to complete my happiness. There is nothing to stop you, for I have heard that your cruel husband is dead. Please do as I ask you, and we will rule together over this great kraal."

The young mother was delighted to accept the offer of so great and noble a Prince, and she did so happily. Now, both she and her children could have a happiness that they had never known before. And of course, all of the people rejoiced, too, for they were to have both a King and a Queen.

The Rabbit Prince

A SHANGANI TALE

ALTHOUGH IT IS NOT A USUAL THING, many years ago
there lived a Rabbit and an Antelope who were very good
friends. The Rabbit was cunning and wise, far more so
than most other animals; but the friend was just an innocent little antelope, who was fond of men and never
strayed from the kraal.

One day the Rabbit approached the Antelope with the
following suggestion: "Let us grow our own mealies and
calabashes, so that we will not have to depend upon the
crops grown by men. I know where there is ground that is
just right for planting."

It sounded like a very smart idea to the Antelope, and

he agreed at once. In no time at all the two friends had
chosen their patches of land, hoed them well, and set in
their mealies, calabashes and ground-nuts. This proved to
be simple enough, for many a time the friends had
watched the neighboring Chief's wives at work in the
fields.

When autumn came, the Antelope viewed his patch of
land with pride, for it was larger than the Rabbit's and the
mealies were taller and finer. This sense of pride soon gave
way to a feeling of anxiety, for one day when the Antelope
went to see how his crops were faring, he discovered that
a great part of them were missing. But look! The Rabbit's
crops were all untouched! And just where did the corn
and nuts come from that the Rabbit picked daily? The
Antelope immediately suspected the tricky Rabbit, and
going to him, accused him of stealing the food.

With great indignation, the Rabbit denied the charge
"I have never touched your lands. The King of Kings has
done it, so you will never be able to catch the thief."

"Then answer me this. Where do you get your mealies?
I can see that they do not come from your own land."

"Well, why do you suppose we live near a kraal?" replied the Rabbit playfully. "I eat the mealies that belong
to the Chief."

The Antelope was not convinced of his friend's innocence, but he went along with the explanation for the
time being. However, it was only a day or two later when
he found that his crops had been attacked again.

"Soon I shall have nothing left," he complained to the Rabbit. "What can I do to stop the thief?"

"Why don't we make a trap?" suggested the Rabbit. "We may be able to catch the culprit ourselves."

And so the clever Rabbit pulled some hairs from a zebra's tail, and with them made a net of slipknots. This he laid on the ground, scattering twigs and earth over the net so that it would remain unnoticed. Then a few mealies were sprinkled about in order to tempt the thief to walk into the trap.

Early the next morning, the Rabbit and the Antelope awoke and together went to the mealie patch to examine the trap. They were delighted to find that the fine black hairs had done their job, for the net held a most beautiful bird. The long wings of the bird were beating ceaselessly, but to no avail. As the Rabbit tried to loosen the knots with his teeth, the Antelope held the bird. But no sooner were the knots untied, than the bird slipped away with one powerful stroke of its wings. High up into the clouds it soared, leaving the Rabbit astonished and the Antelope downcast.

"Never mind," comforted the Rabbit, "we will set the trap again tonight."

And so they did, and on the next day they returned to find that the beautiful bird had been caught once again in the long line of knots. This time however, she was not alone, for a great flock of anxious birds circled about her. The birds watched as the Rabbit and the Antelope carefully untied the knots and then carried the bird to their hut, lightly bound so that there was no chance of escape. Once they could examine her closely, the friends realized that the most remarkable thing about her was the very long feather in one of her wings. Convinced that this was the source of her strength, the Rabbit grabbed the feather and plucked it out of the wing; and to the great astonishment of both friends, the bird turned into a beautiful Princess!

Overcome with pleasure, the cunning Rabbit beseeched the lovely maiden to remain in the hut, assuring her that she would be well-fed and well-treated. And all the while he spoke, he was busy hiding the feather.

The Princess had no choice. Having lost her feather, she could no longer return to her home in the clouds, and so she agreed to stay in the hut. Every day the flock of birds flew to the door of the hut to ask her when she was coming home again.

"Have patience," she beseeched them. "I will return at the right time."

"Where is your long feather?" they chirped. "Have you lost it?"

"Don't worry, it is quite safe," she assured them. "The Rabbit has put it away."

And that is the way things went along for many days. The more the Princess saw of the Rabbit, the more she admired his wisdom and cunning. "What a pity," she thought, "that he is only a rabbit! There is no Chief in all

of my father's lands who can compare with his cleverness."
And then, since the Princess was a Fairy who had magic
powers, she decided that the Rabbit should remain a
Rabbit no longer.

On the following day when the Princess and the Rabbit
were alone, he asked her, "Do you know who took your
feather?"

"Yes," she answered promptly, "you took it."

"You are quite right." He seemed surprised. "But do
you know where I put it?"

"No," replied the Princess, "but that does not matter,
for I am quite sure that it is safe with you. I want you to
keep it, but first allow me to see it once more, just for a
moment."

She was so beautiful that the Rabbit could deny her
nothing. He brought out the feather, and in a twinkling
she had snatched it out of his hand. To his amazement,
however, she did not attempt to fly away, but instead
threw the feather back to him, laughing all the while.

As soon as the feather touched him, the Rabbit turned
into a handsome Prince, and the Princess's joy knew no
bounds. No one, however, was more delighted than the
Rabbit himself, for this transformation had radically
changed his prospects in regard to the Princess. He could
now woo her as an equal, even though he had no lands to
offer her. Although this latter did not present a problem
to the wily Rabbit, for he reasoned that being a man now,
he could certainly kill the little Antelope and thereby add

to his property that of his friend. Which is exactly what he did. After he had slain the Antelope he came back to the Princess saying, "Can I hope that you will marry me now?"

"Yes, indeed, but let us keep it a secret. The birds who come from my home must never hear of it, for my parents would never allow me to marry an earth man."

In the meantime the flock of birds became tired of waiting for the Princess, and they thought, "The Princess will never return to her home, now that she has the Rabbit Prince. We will never see our home in the sky again, unless we can kill him." So convinced were they of this, that they consulted with a Mouse and a Woodpecker, who were considered to be the wisest magicians in that country. Their advice was to put a safe poison in the Prince's food. This would put him to sleep for a few weeks, and the Princess, supposing him dead, would return to her home. However, the Princess found out about the plot, and she warned the Prince in good time. As a result, the Rabbit Prince ate nothing and escaped his fate. The surprising part of this episode, was that the Mouse and the Woodpecker became so fond of the Prince, that they refused to give any more advice that might harm him. If anything, they vowed that they would do what they could to help him instead.

Eventually, though there did come a day when the Princess longed to go home again. And she asked the Prince, "Would you like to see my father and mother?"

"Very much," he replied. "But where can we find them?"

"They live in the sky," she answered. "But first you must go and fetch me the feather."

Once again the Rabbit Prince got the feather, and the Princess placed it on the ground. As soon as she did so, it began to grow taller and taller until at last it reached into the clouds. At once they began to climb, the Prince and the Princess going first, followed by the Mouse and the Woodpecker who insisted upon coming along to protect the Prince. Higher and higher they climbed, through the clouds and then beyond them. Finally they reached an enormous cave whose mouth was closed by a great stone. At sight of this, the Princess fell into a state of despair. "How can we ever roll that stone aside?" she cried.

"There is nothing that I cannot nibble through," said the Mouse. "Let me see what I can do." He nibbled as hard as he could at the edge of the stone, but with no success at all.

Then the Woodpecker stepped forth saying, "Let me try. I make my nest in wood, and my beak can enter very hard surfaces." So saying, she tapped carefully all around the edge of the great stone and suddenly cried out: "This is the way to do it!" She had found a tiny knob on one side of the stone, no longer than a finger. This she pulled, and the stone rolled back, revealing the mouth of the cave.

No sooner had they started to enter the cave, when they became aware of a huge monster blocking their way. Two horns rose out of his head, and dangling from each of them, was the head of a human being. There were eyes all over his body, from his toe to his head, and from every eye glared a bright green light. Without hesitating for one minute, the Princess drew out the long feather and dug it right into his face; and of all things, the monster vanished like a puff of smoke.

"Now," proclaimed the Princess, "we can proceed safely at last." They walked through the entire cave until they came to the other end, which looked out on a world much the same as our own. This was the Princess's home, and she ran toward it joyfully. There her mother and father as well as their people, crowded around her full of rejoicing.

When the first greetings were over, the Rabbit Prince was noticed by her parents. "Where did you get this man from?" they asked her.

"Oh," she said, laughing, "I have stolen him from the earth."

Her father did not laugh; instead he frowned. He was proud of the fact that he never had anything to do with earth people. For in truth he feared them. His anger became even more apparent when the Princess revealed that the Rabbit Prince was her chosen husband. Despite her father's rage, the princess, continued to plead for her lover, telling her parents of his wisdom and power, his cleverness and his nobility. All of this made no impression on the old Chief, who insisted that no daughter of the clouds had ever married a man from the earth, or ever would.

The Princess still clung to the Prince and refused to send him away, despite her father's commands that he be returned to the earth. So the Chief groped for a way to rid himself of the despised Prince and finally decided that he would have to be killed if he could not be banished.

The Chief's first idea was to trick the Rabbit Prince at a big feast of welcome. Many days were spent preparing the food; and while the food was being cooked, the little Mouse ran all over, nibbling on savory morsels. Then on the morning of the feast day, the little Mouse saw that the food for all the guests was placed in dishes, but the Prince's portion was put into two little black pots. When no one was looking but the Mouse, a strangely dressed old woman came forth. She looked very like a witch, and sure enough she sprinkled some powder on the food that was meant for the Prince.

Soon the feast began, but before the Prince had a chance to eat, the little Mouse ran up his back and whispered in his ear: "Eat none of the food that was prepared for you; only drink the beer, for that is the one safe thing."

The Prince heeded this advice, and thus escaped the first danger.

Having failed to kill the Prince with their plan, the people of the Clouds were naturally disappointed. But they did not give up. They assembled anew, armed with their greatest magicians, to make fresh plans. "We will arrange for a hailstorm of the greatest magnitude," offered these wise men. "Let the Prince go out on the great plains tomorrow, and we will see that he does not come back alive."

And so the very next morning, the King of the Sky sent the Rabbit Prince on a journey to another kraal across the wide plains. After he had traveled for about three hours and was many miles from any shelter, great clouds suddenly appeared on the horizon. These were of the deepest blue-black, and they fanned out until the sun was completely covered. Then from the distance came a continuously louder rumble of thunder. It never ceased for a moment; and the sound was ever sharper and more threatening as it came closer and closer. "That is not thunder," said the Prince, "it is hail, and there is no shelter for miles. I fear that I shall never live to see the Princess again."

He was very close to despair when he heard a voice at his ear. "Do not fear," said the Woodpecker. "Just lie down on the ground. The Princess has given me her feather, and I will protect your head with it."

So the Prince did as he was told and lay down, with the little Woodpecker spreading her wings and hovering over his head with the feather in her mouth. One great hailstone landed, as if shot from a gun, and then another and another. They came by the hundreds and thousands, as large as fowls' eggs, jagged and icy-cold, with a sound like the roar of countless torrents over endless precipices. Such a storm had never been known before.

When the Prince returned to the King of the Sky, safe and unharmed, his enemies were more dumbfounded and enraged than ever. But yet they were persistent. Holding a great indaba under a shady tree, they consulted all of their chief men and magicians and they all came to the same conclusion. A royal hunt that would last for many days would be ordered, and during that time the Prince would be killed with an assegai. This of course would be accomplished as if by accident, for no one wanted the Princess to suspect that her husband had been murdered. This time they felt that they could not fail, for there would be countless opportunities to shoot the Prince in the heat of the chase.

Unseen in the boughs of that shady tree, sat the Wood-pecker, overhearing everything. Being a wise bird, as well as a magician, she understood what must be done. Flying to the empty hut of the first wizard of the sky, she mixed together the fat of the deadly mamba snake with the fat of the python. To this she added some skin taken from a tiger. These she put together and then placed the mixture in three little bags of pythonskin. With the bags in her mouth, she returned to the Rabbit Prince.

"Take these," she commanded, "and carry them at all times. New dangers threaten your life."

The Prince happily obeyed his faithful friend and then proceeded to the hunt as he had been directed. For many days they all remained on the hunt, and on each one of those days, someone made an attempt on the Prince's life, but to no avail. All of the assegais hurled toward him dropped powerless to the ground, for the charms that the Woodpecker had given him made him invulnerable.

Returning home safe and sound once more, the Prince knew only one thing: it was useless to struggle any longer, for the people in the sky would never rest until they had killed him. These feelings he told to his bride.

The Princess listened in silence and in sorrow. Then she said, "You are quite right. I had hoped that they would see in time how clever and brave you are, but it is no use. Let us steal away tonight and seek our fortune on the earth below. Go and call our friends the Mouse and the Woodpecker while I get the ladder ready."

While the Prince was gone, the Princess took out the magic feather and this time she pointed it downward toward the earth. Immediately it began growing, and in a few minutes the point reached the Rabbit Prince's hut. Then the four of them climbed down, leaving the Land of Clouds forever.

Once they were back on the earth, a meeting was called of the four friends. "Something must be done to find men to serve under us," said the Prince. "I want a Kingdom and cattle for my Princess; I cannot allow her to live like this any longer."

"My dear Prince, you have only to wish and all will be given to you. Those three little bags of charms will do whatsoever you command." So spoke the Woodpecker.

"If that is true," retorted the Prince, "let there appear beautiful huts, strong maidens to serve the Princess, and the wisest of women to advise her."

And right away there appeared the most perfect huts imaginable, filled with everything the Princess could want. In front of them stood thirty strong girls and a majestic old Queen, who knew everything a wise woman is supposed to know.

Sure that his wife would be safe and well cared for, the Rabbit Prince left her with the Woodpecker, while he and the Mouse went forth in quest of soldiers and cattle. The air everywhere was full of talk of a mighty King who possessed warriors and cattle by the thousands. By using the little bags of charms, the Prince hoped to convince many of these warriors, along with their cattle, to leave this Chief and follow him instead. This venture met with the greatest of luck, for many of the warriors and cattle did follow him back to his Princess.

Then at last he was able to establish a great kingdom, and to reward his two friends, the Woodpecker and the Mouse, as they justly deserved. The Mouse, he changed into a Prince and the Woodpecker into a Princess. I am sorry that I do not remember all of the adventures that followed this, but I do recall that the Mouse became a great Chief, and that to this day both he and his wife, the Princess, are devoted to the Rabbit Prince.

The Fairy Bird

A SWAZI TALE

Ever so many years ago, there lived a boy named
Duma, who had a sister four years younger named
Dumasane. Both had been born in the summertime during
great storms, and so they had been named "the children of
Duma the thunder."

Their parents were poor, so poor that they owned no
herds or cattle; but nevertheless the children lived happily
in the parents' tiny kraal at the foot of a mountain. The
only food they had came from the fields, which they
worked themselves; and when one of the family longed
for a calabash of thick milk, his wish was in vain. For they
were so poor that they could not even buy a goat.

One year as the sun grew warmer and the spring rains started arriving, the whole family went forth to hoe their lands. "Let us try some new ground today," suggested the father, "for the old lands are becoming poor, and there is still plenty of rich soil further down in the valley."

Saying this, he started walking down the narrow path, followed by his wife, Duma, and Dumasane, each one carrying a pick. Soon they came to a fertile piece of land, so smooth and level and free from stones, that they began to work immediately at turning the sods. They labored until sundown, and only then did they return to their hut, tired but happy from their day's work. They felt they had done a great deal. So it was with great confusion that they saw the next morning that all of the sods they had turned the day before had been turned back into their old places; and the ground was as smooth and level as if they had never set foot on it.

Once again they began to work, and by the end of the day they had again prepared a large piece of land for sowing. But on the following day, they found that the same thing had happened; not a sign remained of the previous day's labors. They continued to work for many days, but every night in the same way their efforts were undone.

"There must be some reason for this," said the father at last. "I will stay here tonight and see what happens."

So that night when the children and his wife went home, the father slipped behind a great rock to watch the newly turned lands. He had not been there very long when he saw a most beautiful bird come out of the bushes and alight on the fresh sods. It was like no bird he had ever seen before, for its feathers were of every color that he had ever imagined; its wings were of scarlet, its tail a metallic blue, and its head a bright gold, which shaded into a bronze-green on its breast. It shone like a jewel in the sun, and its beauty radiated over the entire field. Flying to the very stone behind which the father lay hidden, it perched on the highest peak. Then spreading its wings, it chirped in a high clear voice:

"Chanchasa! Chanchasa! Kilhisa!"

And at the very instant that these words were uttered, every sod in the field turned over, and no one could ever have guessed that any work had ever been done there. The father remained very quiet throughout this, waiting for the bird to come within arm's reach. When it did, he snatched at it suddenly!

"Now!" he exclaimed, "I have you! You are clever enough to undo my work, so it is only fair that you should provide me with a meal." And he prepared to wring its neck.

"No, no! Spare me!" cried the bird. "If you will only spare my life, I will provide you with cream, fresh milk, curds and whey, all of your days!"

The man opened his eyes at this offer and replied, "I can see now that you must be a Fairy Bird, and if what you say is true, then I will keep you alive."

Holding the bird firmly, the man started for home. When he reached the gate of the kraal, he called to his wife to send the children out while the evening meal was being prepared. As soon as the man was alone with his wife, he closed the door of the hut and showed her the bird.

"What good will a bird do us?" she asked him suspiciously.

"You will soon see," said her husband. And taking the sack of woven grass that they used for straining their beer, he hung it up in the middle of the hut and put the bird inside. Then he took a great calabash and held it up, (for only a man is permitted to harvest the food provided by beasts) and he called upon the bird to fulfill its promise.

"Chanchasa! Chanchasa! Kilhisa!" called the bird in its high voice, flapping its wings.

As it cried out, the calabash started filling up with cream, then with sweet milk and finally with curdled milk, as much as could be used in one day. The wife was delighted, for the cream would keep their karosses in the most beautiful condition, and the milk would make the children big and strong.

"Do not tell anyone about this bird," she whispered to

her husband, "for he is far too wonderful! He must stay here in the sack, and we will not even let the children see how we get the milk and cream."

And that very night, they all feasted well. The next day they went out with hoe in hand, light of heart and merry in song:

> *"Now we have cream and milk,*
> *Fresh milk and curds and whey;*
> *Now we go a-working*
> *Singing merrily every day."*

Every night after that Duma and Dumasane were given a big bowl of curds, and this puzzled them very much. Where had it come from? There was neither flock nor herd within many miles, and yet there was cream, fresh milk and curdled milk every day, such as there had never been before.

"I think I know where it comes from," confided Dumasane to her brother one day. "They must get it from the hut itself, for it is never brought here. And it always appears after they have been there alone."

"Perhaps you are right. Suppose we look through the thatch of the hut this evening," replied Duma. "I know where there is an opening in the wall that will let us see everything that happens."

That night they both waited for the opportunity to watch; and when it came, they saw the Fairy Bird come out of his sack, flap his wings and fill each calabash to the brim. They saw it through eyes filled with wonder, and they were so excited that sleep did not come easily afterward.

On the next morning, the parents were forced to leave the children alone in the kraal while they made a long journey to see a relative. As they left, joyful songs caressed their lips about their new found prosperity:

"Now we have cream and milk,
Fresh milk, and curds and whey."

The wife sang even louder than her husband, for now that she was as rich as any of her neighbors, she was full of well-deserved pride.

When they came back at dusk, they were tired and looking forward to their evening meal. However at the kraal a most dreadful sight met their eyes! The whole place was swimming in milk and cream, and though the sack still hung in the middle of the hut, it was empty. At the outer gate, the boy and girl stood crying so bitterly that it was some time before they could confess their deed.

"It is all our fault," they sobbed. "We always wondered what you did all alone in the hut, and last night we looked through the thatch and saw everything. As soon as you left this morning, we took the bird down and told him to say 'Chanchasa.' But the milk and cream came so fast that we feared we would be drowned, and in our fright, we let the bird fly away."

Upon hearing this, the parents were enraged. "You have

brought starvation back upon us," cried the mother. "We can no longer keep you here; you must be punished!"

With this, she lifted the children, one in each arm, and carried them to a big ravine on a nearby mountainside and pushed them down. In her anger, she felt justified in leaving them to fend for themselves for a few days.

When the children reached the bottom of the ravine, they realized that they were in a deep narrow valley, which penetrated into the heart of the mountains. Great trees in full leaf almost shut out the sun, and a clear stream ran along the entire bottom, amid tall ferns and flowering bushes. For two days the children wandered around, and on the third, they came upon a bush laden with delicious berries, which they ate.

"Now," began Duma, for he was the older and the wiser, "we can no longer remain here waiting for our parents to forgive us. We must seek a new home, in case they have forsaken us. Let us walk to the top of this valley and perhaps we shall find a kraal where we can get some food."

Dumasane agreed with her brother, and both children set off at once, following the flow of the stream and singing as they went:

> *"We are the foolish children,*
> *Who lost the Fairy Bird*
> *Which gave our father cream,*
> *Fresh milk, curds and whey.*
> *A-lack-a-day."*

These words were sung to a sad little tune, and they caused Dumasane to weep bitterly, for they reminded her of the pleasant home that was no longer theirs. Climbing higher, they came to the top of the creek, which was marked with a great towering tree, covered with the blackest of berries. Leaving their song unfinished, they rushed to pluck the berries from the bowing tree; but before they could pick even one, all of the berries became a great flock of tiny blackbirds, crying shrilly as they flew from the tree. At the head of the procession, bright as a flower and gay as ever, winged the Fairy Bird himself.

Seeing the children, he flew back to the tree and perched himself on the lowest bough, but only after listening to their tale of woe, did he speak.

"I see that you are in difficulty because of me and that all of your troubles started after you gave me my freedom," he said. "So I will not forsake you now, even as you did not forsake me then." And he snapped a twig from the tree and gave it to them, saying:

"Take this stick and walk in that direction until you come to a huge rock. Go around the rock, and as you do, strike it with the stick and say these words:

> "My mother's and father's cattle were killed.
> They say we have done great wrong,
> For we have lost the Fairy Bird
> Which gave us cream and milk,
> Fresh milk and curds and whey,
> Stone, stone, open in two,

So that we can go in.
Father and mother cast us out,
There is no milk and curds and whey.
We have done wrong, we have done wrong.
Stone, Stone, open in two.
Vula, Etye."

"After this cry, Chanchasa! Chanchasa! Kilhisa! All the time you walk, keep striking the stick against the rock, and when you touch the right place, a door will fly open. Inside of the rock you will find a home, a place where you can live until the time when you are grown up. Everything will be there that you could possibly want, but there is one thing that you must always remember. Never leave a morsel of fat on the fire; if you do, great evil will come of it." And so saying, he rested.

Eagerly the children took the stick, Duma holding it and Dumasane following him, all of her tears forgotten. Obeying the Fairy Bird's directive, they walked until they came in sight of a most immense rock, which stood surrounded by the tallest and greenest of grasses. Never had they seen a rock of such immense size, and after examining it carefully, they walked around it singing the little song and striking it with the fairy stick.

Just as the bird had promised, a little door swung open, without warning, to disclose a huge cave. And though it was a cave, it was more beautifully furnished than any hut the children had ever seen or even imagined; for a king could have made it his home. There were finely woven mats to sleep on and little wooden pillows, most daintily carved. Great fur rugs were piled high to keep the cold away, and there were special things for each child as well. For Dumasane there were beautiful beaded necklaces and girdles. For Duma there was a bow and arrows, the bow strung with pythonskin; and there was a long curly koodoo horn to blow on; and there were the most perfect assegais. For both children, there were lovely skin cloaks, covered with beads.

All around the walls of the cave stood pots and calabashes of shining red and black, filled with cream, fresh milk and curdled milk, as well as delicious porridge, which was already cooked. Besides all of this, there were great baskets full of corn, nuts and maize. It was apparent that there was enough food here for months to come.

The two children looked at each other, and the words that they spoke were the same; "This is the loveliest place that I have ever seen. I am not afraid to be here, and I think I will be happy."

And so they were. Many years went by, and Duma became a fine young man, and Dumasane, the prettiest girl that you can imagine. There was always plenty to eat, for every day the calabashes and baskets were filled anew, even faster than the children could empty them. There were no troubles, and they led a free and happy life; Dumasane learning to cook and keep house, while Duma became an expert huntsman. There came a time, however, when they found that their food supply was no longer being replenished, and then they knew that the time had come to work for themselves.

"I will stay and care for the house, while you go hunting for the meat to cook," Dumasane told her brother.

"Very well," he agreed, "but remember, you must take great pains not to leave any fat on the fire. The Fairy Bird warned us that great harm would come if this should happen."

On the first day Dumasane was left alone, she was very careful, and this was true on the second day too. But on the third, she left a bit of fat smouldering on the flame. Not noticing it she set to work rearranging the cooking pots. Then suddenly she heard heavy footsteps hurrying up the path and two deep bass voices booming, "Hum, hoom! Hum, hoom!" Instantly her heart filled with terror! The next minute the door flew open, and there stood an Inzimu and his wife, two monsters most dreadful to behold. They stood upright, and she could see that their feet and hands were like those of a human, but there the similarity ended. For their bodies were covered with flesh that bulged out in huge bumps, and long red hair was sprinkled in clumps over their skin. Their closely set eyes, and mouths that extended from ear to ear, gaping with sharp teeth, made them grotesque to behold. The woman was even uglier than the man, for while he had two horns growing out of his head, she had one right in the middle of her forehead, as well as a long snout like that of a wolf. Both of them had long tails, as long as an elephant's trunk, and with these they could suck up anything they wanted.

Dumasane was terrified, for as soon as she could think

clearly, she realized that they were cannibals. The monsters walked directly into the cave, squinting their tiny eyes, and grunting with every step.

"Take everything in the cave!" pleaded Dumasane, "But please spare me!"

"That would be foolish," they chuckled, "for you have magic power, and you will be able to get all of these things for us and even more."

And in spite of her entreaties and tears, they carried her away. When her brother returned that afternoon, he found the cave empty of all its furnishings and no sign of his sister. Sitting down in deep despair, he imagined her dead.

Suddenly, the Fairy Bird, splendidly arrayed in gold and scarlet, flew into the cave. "Do not grieve," he begged Duma, "but take this stick and bag and go deep into the bush. As you walk, wave the stick before you, and every stinging insect that you meet will fly into the open bag. When it is filled, return and hang the bag up in the middle of the cave."

Duma did just as the Fairy Bird had bid him; and as he waved the stick, every deadly thing within call came and took its place in the bag. There were no less than two great black mambas, there were scorpions and big hairy spiders, fierce little black bees, great yellow wasps, hornets and clouds of poisonous mosquitoes, newly hatched and very venomous. When the bag was filled to its brim, Duma returned and hung it in the middle of the cave. Then he sat down to await what would happen.

It was not long before he heard the Inzimus singing, "Hum, hoom!" "Hum! Hoom!" and tramping with their heavy footsteps. The door flew open, and they beheld Duma.

"Ah, let us take the boy, too," said the Inzimu, "for he will be useful to us."

"And look," shrieked his wife. "There is a bag that we overlooked! No doubt it is full of good things to eat."

Pulling down the bag, they could hardly wait to see what good things lay within. But as they opened it, they unloosed all manner of poisonous animals and insects, which attacked them unmercifully. Snakes and scorpions crawled up their legs, while bees and mosquitoes encircled their heads, joined by wasps who deafened them with angry cries. Screaming wildly, the two monsters fled, running down the ravine, stumbling over thorny bushes and great rocks. They did not stop until they had plunged into the depths of a pool in order to escape their assailants. But even there they found no relief, for no sooner would they lift their heads for a breath of air then they were attacked anew by the mob of venomous creatures. In the end, both monsters died, and Duma, who had watched it all, was safe at last.

Now the Fairy Bird told Duma to return to the cave, where he would be reunited with Dumasane. And as the bird had promised, she was waiting for him there. They embraced warmly, each one telling the other what had happened during their separation. They rested a bit, then finally went outside the cave, where the Fairy Bird waited to speak with them.

"This is the last time that you will see me. Before leaving, I am going to change both of you into royal birds. Thus you will be able to find a better home than I can give you now, for you are no longer children. Do not fear for your future, for only a King will have the right to own you."

With this, the Fairy Bird took flight, his colors flashing in the sunlight. And it was true, they never did see him again; but they themselves had become two beautiful green lorys with scarlet and black wings and a great green crest edged with white on their heads. To tell the truth, they were almost as lovely as the Fairy Bird himself. Living was easy for them now; they fed on nuts and fruits, and the clear river pools were their baths, both morning and evening.

Just at that time there was a great King who reigned over the land where the two birds lived. One day the Queen of the country sent an Induna out to cut wood, and he returned from the forest with an incredible story. He told of chopping at the foot of a tree and overhearing human voices singing in the upper branches. As he listened he heard a song:

> *"We were once a boy and girl;*
> *We let our father's bird go free*
> *Which gave us both cream and milk,*

Fresh milk and curds and whey,
Now we live alone in the trees."

Then, as he looked up into the branches, he saw two beautiful green lorys. "Those are royal birds," he had muttered to himself; "some great witchcraft is at work here." So he had returned to the Queen, who was a wise woman, and told her the whole story.

"Such a thing is possible," said the Queen, "but we shall go and see for ourselves."

So the Induna took his Queen and all the Princesses back into the forest and brought them to the foot of the tree. Once again, he began to chop, and once more the birds began to sing. Their song convinced the Queen that these were indeed enchanted creatures. Whereupon she commanded the Induna to climb the tree and catch the pair of lorys for her.

The Induna climbed the tree, as the Queen had ordered, and holding his hands out under the broad green leaves, he waited for the birds to come within reach. As soon as they did, he snatched them and brought them down to the waiting Queen.

No sooner had he placed the pair of birds in the Queen's hands, then they changed into a most beautiful young man and woman. They were brought at once before the King, who listened to their many adventures with great atonishment. However when they had finished, the King had a surprise for them too.

"You have an uncle who is a great Chief. His lands lie

next to mine. I shall bring you to him."

And so Duma and Dumasane were brought to
home, where they soon made many good friend
Queen of their uncle was especially fond of Dur
and she arranged for her to marry her own son. Du
well also, for he married one of the Queen's daught
became a great Chief in his own right.

Baboon-Skins

A SWAZI TALE

Now in this story there is neither Fairy nor Inzimu; there is no one who wins a kingdom with secret spells. (Some little bags of pythonskin are mentioned, but you will see that they have no effect on anyone.) In fact the only magic used in this story is a woman's wit and kindness of heart; the oldest charms in the world.

Many years ago there lived a Chief who had many wives. Two of these were more distinguished than the others for each had a most beautiful daughter. In fact these two wives had families exactly alike, for each had a plain son too. I cannot tell you what became of the plain sons, though no doubt each had a history, for this tale concerns only the two beautiful daughters.

124

The name of one girl was Inkosesana, which means "the Young Lady." Her mother was very proud of her and expected her to marry a great Chief, and Inkosesana was as conceited as possible as a result of this.

The name of the other maiden was Lalhiwe, which means "Thrown Away." As you can imagine from her name, she was a much quieter and more modest girl than Inkosesana.

As time went on and both maidens grew into womanhood, suitors began to arrive. Each mother was hoping for great things for her daughter, and the rivalry between the two families became more and more bitter. It was all they could do to keep their constant quarrels from reaching the ears of the Chief.

Early one morning Lalhiwe's mother awoke and went to prepare corn for the day's food. To her horror, she discovered some animal blood and small pythonskin bags, filled with charms, under the grinding stone.

"Lalhiwe!" she cried out, "come and see what bad fortune awaits us; cast your eyes upon this!"

Lalhiwe rushed to her mother and upon seeing the charms she nearly fainted. "It is witchcraft!" she said. "It must be some wickedness devised by Inkosesana and her mother. They will never rest until we come to harm. I know in my heart that these charms are meant to cast a spell over us so that we may fall ill and die."

Lalhiwe's mother nodded her head in agreement. And after a minute she begged Lalhiwe to run quickly to a neighbor, who was a Wise Woman, and to bring her back with the charms necessary to undo the evil that their rivals had intended for them.

After this had been accomplished, Lalhiwe sat down and spoke to her mother, saying, "Mother, I am tired of all this. How can I care about beauty when it has brought us only endless quarrels and bitter jealousies? To end this constant fighting, I have decided to cover myself with baboon skins, the ugliest skins of all. I shall wrap myself up in them and remain that way until Inkosesana has married. In that way, we shall all have peace."

That very day she asked her brother to fetch two baboon skins for her and to bring them with the heads and the limbs still on them. As soon as they were brought, she joined the two skins at the shoulders and at the heads. Then she slipped into them so that the two heads completely covered her own head. Only her two bright eyes peeped out through the eyeholes she had cut. The rest of her face was completely hidden, and all that one could see was the mask of a grinning ape. The two skins hung down from her shoulders to her knees, in the back and in the front, but one could still see her legs which were pretty and well-shaped. She looked like a person suffering from some great deformity of the head or body, who had hidden herself from the gaze of men.

As soon as her rival's mother heard what Lalhiwe had done, she laughed heartily and said, "This is the best news I have heard for many a long day. What a fool that girl must be! Surely she must be mad!"

And with this opinion, all of the women in the kraal

agreed. For they had never heard of hiding a pretty face before, and it was impossible for them to believe that Lalhiwe would do this in order to find peace. But in spite of all their attempts to convince Lalhiwe of her error, she remained faithful to her idea. She wore the ugly baboon skins every day, and not once did she show her face, even to her dearest friends. Happily, her sacrifice proved to be worthwhile; for after the first few days, peace reigned in the kraal. There were no more quarrels, everyone seemed happier, and Inkosesana became the undisputed beauty of the countryside.

Then one day, many months after Lalhiwe had started wearing the baboon skins, there was a great stir in the kraal. Two ambassadors had arrived from a very mighty Chief, seeking not one bride but two for their master. Both girls must be beautiful, for the Chief was very rich and he was prepared to give a magnificent marriage gift for each of the maidens. The two ambassadors sat and conversed with the head of the kraal, while the women stood in small groups talking excitedly. Finally they were asked to come forward and the request of the great Chief was made known to them.

The mother of Inkosesana was the first to advance. She moved forward with an air of triumph. "Here," she proclaimed, "is the bride that you are searching for," and she brought forth Inkosesana, who did indeed look beautiful. She had thrown aside her cloak, and she stood there decked in all her prettiest beads, which set off her lovely black skin and graceful figure to full advantage. The am-

127

bassadors both agreed at once: "This is the most beautiful girl we have seen as yet. We accept her with pleasure, for we believe that our King could not wish for a more lovely maiden." Then turning to the Chief they asked, "Have you another pretty daughter, so that we may see her too?"

The Chief did not answer, but the mother of Inkosesana, made bold with pride and longing to triumph yet further above her rival, called out, "Yes, there is another daughter, but she is always wrapped in baboon skins and she is of no importance at all."

"Let us see her anyway," insisted the ambassadors, whose curiosity was aroused by this bit of information.

And so Lalhiwe was brought forth, holding her skins tightly around her body. But though she was covered with baboon skins, nothing could take away from the grace of her movements; and the King's messengers walked around her, longing to see her hidden face.

"Why are you hiding underneath those skins?" they asked her. "You have very pretty legs and you walk gracefully. What is wrong with you that you do not wish to show your face? We beg you to let us see your true appearance."

"No," replied Lalhiwe. "He who marries me, must marry me for myself alone and not for my beauty."

"Are you deformed then? Or are you so very ugly?"

"I did not say that," answered Lalhiwe. "All I said was that he who marries me must marry me for myself alone."

"But why is it that you behave so strangely?"

"To please myself," retorted Lalhiwe.

"I cannot believe that you are not deformed," said one of the men, hoping to arouse her anger.

"You may believe what you wish, but I tell you the truth," repeated the girl; and although the ambassadors did all they could to provoke her into throwing off the skins, she did not get angry nor speak rudely to them.

Finally they realized that they could not make her reveal herself, and they held a conference with each other. Should they take Lalhiwe as well as the beautiful Inkosesana and risk the King's displeasure? True, they had both admired her wit and her good temper, but what was to be found underneath the skins? In a moment of weakness they decided to take a chance, and they asked for Lalhiwe also, praying that all would be well in the end.

Before returning to their King, the ambassadors went to the brothers of both maidens. The brother of Inkosesana they instructed to make a big kraal to receive the cattle in payment for his sister, as there was no doubt that their master would be delighted with her. To Lalhiwe's brother they said very little, aside from directing him to send his sister to their master. This brother, fearing that his sister would not be welcomed, did not bother to make a kraal at all for a marriage gift.

The messengers then returned to their King, who was delighted with the reports that they brought of Inkosesana. However, when he heard the tale of the second bride, the one who wore baboon skins, he became enraged. "No girl," he shouted, "who has a pretty face would ever hide it. I am certain that she must be absolutely hideous; and remember, if that is the case, you shall both pay the penalty of death. I cannot believe that I sent such fools on such an important mission!"

The ambassadors now regretted what they had done. They were terrified lest the second bride be hideous, for the King always kept his word. And while he awaited the arrival of the brides, the King sent twenty cattle for each one of them, less than was suitable; "We can easily send more if both are acceptable," said he; "and if they should not be, for I will not have an ugly bride, we shall not have to ask for a return of the marriage gift. The forty cattle will be proper payment for Inkosesana."

At the appointed time, the two brides said farewell to their kraal and set out on their journey together. They walked for many days, each attended by her own bridesmaids. Finally they reached their destination and were brought at once to the great Chief. With Inkosesana, he was pleased immediately; but at Lalhiwe, who still remained covered in her baboon skins, he looked with puzzled eyes. Noticing her graceful bearing, he began to admire her, longing to know her secret.

"I beg of you, my maiden," said he, "please let me see your face."

"No, great King," answered Lalhiwe in her usual quiet voice; "I cannot show my face to anyone until the wedding morning." And that was her last word on the matter.

The two brides then retired with their maids, each to her own hut, until all preparations for the wedding feast were completed. Among the women in the King's kraal,

130

there was great gossip. For Inkosesana there was nothing but admiration, while for Lalhiwe there was only scorn for one who could be nothing but hideous. "She is undoubtedly the most ugly of women," they decided, "or she would surely show her face."

When the day of the wedding arrived, each bride left her hut and went down to the river to bathe. Since they went to separate pools, neither one could see the other.

Lalhiwe and her maids descended to a deep pool underneath a great rock, where it was pleasantly warm from the morning sun. Tall white lilies grew on the banks and fresh green ferns peeped out of every nook and cranny. Slipping off her baboon skins, Lalhiwe rolled them into a tight bundle and buried them in an animal hole near the pool. Then she and her maidens laughed and chattered as they bathed in the clear pool, until the time came to array themselves for the wedding.

The bridesmaids decked themselves in their most beautiful beadwork; but Lalhiwe, as was the custom for a bride on her wedding morning, wore a skirt of deep black oxskins, the dress that was worn by married women. For an ornament, she wore just a girdle of bleached white beads encircling her waist, and in her hand she held an assegai. Though her dress was simple, when she stood there in the dazzling sun, her maidens cried out, "Lalhiwe! You are infinitely more beautiful than you ever were! Indeed, you are far more lovely than Inkosesana."

And they were telling her the truth. For all of the months that Lalhiwe had been hidden from the sun, her beauty had increased; her skin had become as smooth and soft as a lily petal, and her every movement was a joy to behold.

The bridesmaids gathered behind Lalhiwe, and together they started up the path toward the kraal. As they walked they sang a song, a sad song of farewell for a friend that would be playing with them no longer in their old home.

As they approached the gate of the kraal, they met Inkosesana and her maidens, who proudly stepped in front so that they could meet the first glances of the

wedding guests. All greeted Inkosesana with great approval, but in truth, their eyes looked beyond her, waiting anxiously to catch the first glimpse of her mysterious sister. When Lalhiwe finally appeared, perfect in every sense, loud shouts of surprise and joy came from all sides.

"She is so lovely!" cried all the guests. "There has never been one so beautiful in our land!"

At last the two brides appeared before the King and danced for him in the great cattle kraal, as was the custom. The King, dumbstruck with amazement, never once took

his eyes from Lalhiwe. As soon as the wedding was over, he called his two ambassadors to him and gave each of them twenty beautiful oxen as a gift of appreciation. "You have shown yourselves to be wise and trustworthy men," he said, "for Lalhiwe is beautiful beyond belief. Choose all of my finest young cattle and send them as a marriage gift to her father. Let the first herd that I sent be the marriage gift for Inkosesana, but make sure that Lalhiwe has a marriage settlement such as has never before been given."

The King's commands were carried out at once by his relieved ambassadors. Lalhiwe's mother, surprised and grateful, rejoiced for many days after the arrival of the marvelous herd of cattle. She, in truth, had never expected that such honor would come upon her child. Her rival, however, the mother of Inkosesana, hid herself in her hut, filled with bitter disappointment that she had not triumphed in the end. She sulked for many months and never again regained her old position in the tribe.

Glossary

ASSEGAI: a small light spear of which natives usually carry several. An assegai can be thrown as a dart or used like a spear at close range.

CALABASH: the name of the gourd or fruit of the Calabash tree. The hollow shell may be used for bowls, pots or other utensils.

GIRDLE: a belt worn around the waist to secure or hold the clothing. It may also be used to carry a weapon, a purse, etc.

IMBULA *or* INZIMU: the same as the ogre of European fairy tales; the Imbula being the female, and the Inzimu, the male. He or she is semi-human and prefers the flesh of man to any other. They have light-colored skins and red hair.

INDABA: a conference or a council.

INDUNA: a head man or leader under the command of a Chief.

KAROSSES: rugs made of skins or of bark, beautifully sewn together.

KOODOO: a kind of antelope with fine horns.

KRAAL: a village of South or Central African natives, consisting of a collection of huts surrounded by a fence.

LOBOLA: the marriage gift presented by the bridegroom to the bride's father. This gift, consisting of cattle, gives him the legal claim to his wife.

MANUMBELA: a bush with bright glossy leaves and silvery stem. The fruit is bright red and grows closely around the stem in great quantities, a little like English holly. The berries are the size of a small plum and are considered very good to eat.

MEALIES: the name generally used in South Africa for Indian corn or maize.

OCHRE: much prized among Kafirs as a dressing for the hair and skin. It is said to protect them from the heat of the sun and is thought to be very becoming. It is a fine colored red clay.

SEDWABA: the name of the full skirt of black oxskins, which no girl wears until her bridal morning, and then continues to wear as a married woman.

THICK MILK: this is maas or mase, a preparation of sour milk. Kafirs never drink fresh milk, but let it stand in special pots until curds have formed.